FAKE GAME

LISA SUZANNE

FAIR GAME
VEGAS ACES BOOK THREE
© 2021 Lisa Suzanne

All rights reserved. In accordance with the US Copyright Act of 1976, the scanning, uploading, and sharing of any part of this book without the permission of the publisher or author constitute unlawful piracy and theft of the author's intellectual property. No part of this book may be reproduced or transmitted in any form or by any means, electronic or mechanical, including photocopying, recording, or by any information storage and retrieval system without the written permission of the author, except where permitted by law and except for excerpts used in reviews. If you would like to use any words from this book other than for review purposes, prior written permission must be obtained from the publisher.

Published in the United States of America by Books by LS, LLC.

ISBN: 9798708663757

This book is a work of fiction. Any similarities to real people, living or dead, is purely coincidental. All characters and events in this work are figments of the author's imagination.

Cover Designed by Najla Qamber Designs
Content Editing by It's Your Story Content Editing
Proofreading by Proofreading by Katie

Fair GAME

BOOKS BY LISA SUZANNE

A LITTLE LIKE DESTINY SERIES
A Little Like Destiny (Book One)
Only Ever You (Book Two)
Clean Break (Book Three)

MY FAVORITE BAND STANDALONES
Take My Heart
The Benefits of Bad Decisions
Waking Up Married
Driving Me Crazy
It's Only Temporary
The Replacement War

Visit Lisa on Amazon for more titles

DEDICATION

To my 3Ms.

CHAPTER 1

I contemplate what to do as I stand in the lobby staring at the closed elevator doors. Watching them close on Jack's face made something snap inside me.

Twenty-six-oh-nine, I repeat in my head, a mantra as I press the call button for another elevator car. *Twenty-six-oh-nine.*

Luke doesn't want me, but Jack seems to. That's where my mind keeps going, an endless loop between twenty-six-oh-nine and Luke doesn't want me.

Twenty-six-oh-nine.

Luke doesn't want me.

And then Jack's voice adds to the mix. *I can promise you a hell of a good time...better than whatever my little brother gives you. Just ask Savannah.*

I can't substitute one Dalton brother for another. It doesn't work like that, though I guess it did for Savannah...and maybe Michelle. I'm not either one of those women, though.

I care about Luke. I love Luke.

So why am I contemplating going up to twenty-six-oh-nine and knocking on the door?

Because *he doesn't love me back.*

That's why. That's what it all comes down to in my head. He hurt me out on that beach with his words. He was so flippant about it when he told me his family didn't need to know that he doesn't have feelings for me as they watch us stand up to be married. So uncaring. So cold.

Is Jack any warmer?

I brush the thought away...but I can't. Not really. Not as the elevator doors glide open and I step on.

I stare at the number board.

Do I hit twenty-seven, the floor where the room I'm sharing with Luke is located?

Or do I press twenty-six instead?

My heart pounds wildly as my fingers seem to take on a mind of their own. They locate a button and press it. It lights up with red behind it, as if to say I'm making the wrong choice. Red equals bad. *Press the other one*, the elevator seems to be saying to me, but I can't make my fingers do it. I stand stock still, alone on the elevator with just my thoughts, but my mind is blank as I stare at the red number board. I don't watch the electronic sign at the top telling me which floor I'm moving past. I keep my eyes trained on that little red circle all the way until the doors pull open.

When I step off, I glance both ways, in part to check which way I'm supposed to go like everyone does when they get off an elevator in a hotel, and in part to make sure the hallway's clear—just to make doubly sure nobody's about to catch me.

Am I doing something wrong? I'm not sure yet...but looking both ways and feeling like I may be caught sure feels like the start of some guilt edging in.

I move toward the room, my heart pounding louder with every step I take down the hall. I look at the numbers posted on each door, counting up by odd numbers until I'm standing outside room twenty-six-oh-nine.

My legs feel like jelly as nerves tingle through me.

Ellie, what the fuck are you doing?

My own conscience screams at me as I lift a fist. My thundering heart races.

Ellie, stop! Turn around. Get back on the elevator. No one ever has to know you walked down this hallway.

Before I can even connect my fist with the wood of the door, it opens.

When it swings open as if by magic or some strange premonition, there stands my future brother-in-law wearing just a pair of athletic shorts that hug his hips.

Either I was staring at the elevator contemplating what to do for a much longer period of time than I realized or he ran up here and basically stripped off his clothes.

He's in peak physical shape with contoured muscles creating the perfect specimen of man. The plane of his chest is solid, his skin smooth and his shoulders broad.

I realize I'm staring directly at his abdomen, but you can't have abs that look like *that* and expect people not to stare.

So I'm attracted to him. Big fucking deal. I'm also attracted to Kristoff from *Frozen*.

And Luke, the tiny voice in my head reminds me. My soon-to-be husband.

Jack opens the door as if to tell me to come in, and I stalk past him. I stop in the middle of his room. It's a suite like ours, with a sitting area and a desk and table here in this room and French doors that are currently wide open to give me a peek into his bedroom. His sheets are a little rumpled, like he's already used the bed.

Did he have sex in here?

With who?

Someone from housekeeping? Someone he picked up in the lobby? He's only been here a few hours, and most of that was spent at dinner. Maybe he works quickly.

It's not my business.

He raises a brow at me. "I had a feeling you'd come."

The first words he speaks to me in this room drip with sex, like he means the word *come* in the carnal sense. My cheeks burn as I try to come up with something witty to say, but words elude me. Sense also apparently eludes me.

Why else would I show up here?

I had sex with Luke the night I met him.

Luke doesn't want me.

His words on the beach ring in my ears.

It's an opportunity.

I get to flaunt my happy ending.

They don't have to know that he doesn't have real feelings.

I stand frozen to the spot for a beat. What now?

I stare at Jack as Luke's words bruise my soul.

Why not have sex with his brother the night I met him, too? Another one-night stand. Another notch in my belt. Another story to tell at the next bachelorette party. I can just picture it now.

Oh, you haven't had two separate one-night stands with a pair of hot brothers? Let me tell you, you haven't lived until you've done that.

I take a step toward him, and he remains in place. The look on his face says *you will come to me* and I'm doing it. I'm moving toward him. Why am I moving toward him?

The answer eludes me, but as my feet shuffle another step in his direction, the gap between us narrows.

My eyes flick to his lips.

What would it be like to kiss him?

He's mesmerizing. Something about Jack Dalton is captivating, and he has the power to make people bend to his will without a single word—as evidenced by the way my feet continue to take small steps to close the space between us.

That tiny voice in my head tells me I'm only even considering this at all because Luke hurt me, but it's not like he'd mind since he basically just told me he doesn't really care about me at all.

I'm spellbound by the man who looks like a slightly older, edgier, tougher version of his younger brother.

A pounding at the door startles me, breaking the spell that holds me in his gaze as a sudden dart of guilt pings through my chest.

My eyes widen as I realize what could've just happened.

Jack's smirk only makes the guilt burn brighter.

I shouldn't be here, and whoever is on the other side of that door is going to get entirely the wrong impression. And I already know who it is before Jack even makes a move toward it to answer it.

I blow out a breath as I brace for the impact.

He doesn't tell me to go hide or move out of sight. He doesn't act like we're doing anything wrong as he starts toward the direction of the knocking.

And so I don't, either.

CHAPTER 2

Jack's eyes lock on mine before he gets all the way to the door, and that's the moment reality comes crashing into me.

How dare he do this to his brother?

How dare *I* do this to his brother?

I wouldn't have kissed him. I wouldn't have done that to Luke.

I repeat that in my head a few times so I believe it.

The steps I was taking toward him were to bring me closer so I could slap him across the face.

I'm attracted to Jack, sure...but I'm in love with Luke. No matter what, I couldn't have really had sex with Jack. I couldn't have done anything with him that might jeopardize the friendship I've built with Luke despite the words he said out on that beach.

I blow out a breath as I force the words that suddenly feel like a desperate attempt to save myself even though they're the truth. "I only came up here to tell you to back down." And maybe to get more details about his involvement with Michelle, but I refrain from mentioning that. I'll circle back to that when the time is right. "I'm marrying your brother, and I'm nothing like Savannah. *Nothing*. So you can get it out of your head right now that something might happen between us."

He laughs, and it's a haughty laugh that plainly says he doesn't believe me and my words won't be enough to shut him up or stop his efforts. "I just want to get to know you," he says. "Did you think I meant something else?"

My cheeks burn, and I hate how he has this *power*. He's a pro at twisting and manipulating, and it's easy to see why the Dalton parents sided with him in whatever went down between the brothers. Luke never stood a chance. He's too nice a guy, while Jack here is reminiscent of a salesman who will do whatever it takes to close the sale. Not a greasy one, or a smarmy or dirty or slimy one, but a devilishly handsome one who probably gets by on his good looks alone most of the time.

"What do you want to know?" I finally ask, my tone exasperated because I can't find it in myself to behave any other way in front of this guy who seems to grate on every last nerve I have at the same time I'm so damn fascinated by him.

Someone is still pounding on the door, but Jack ignores it in favor of this conversation. It has to be Luke on the other side and when he finds me in here—particularly after it's taking so long for Jack to open the door—he will get the wrong impression.

But something compels me to have this conversation anyway.

He narrows his eyes at me. "Why is Luke marrying you?"

My brows dip. "Don't you mean why am *I* marrying *Luke*?"

His gaze on me is hot and intimidating. "I meant what I said."

Because he needs an out so Michelle can't trap him and to shut up Savannah. Because he wants to show his boss he's committed to someone who isn't Michelle. Because he *has* to follow through with it now that it's out in the media because if he doesn't, it'll look like he made it up to get the woman who's carrying his child to back off and that'll just make him look like a douchebag, won't it? Even if it's the truth...

"Because he loves me."

The words sound fake even to my own ears. I can't force them with any shred of authenticity when he just told me he doesn't and my heart is so freshly bruised.

Jack shakes his head. "You may think I don't know my little brother, but I know him. Maybe better than anyone. He isn't marrying you for love." He points a long finger in my direction. "That much I know."

"I don't know what you're talking about."

He ends the conversation there as he keeps his eyes on mine, and I know he ended it there to leave me a bundle of exposed nerves.

He succeeded. Is he going to come after us? Is he going to blow our cover?

Is he going to continue trying to seduce me? And am I strong enough to keep pushing him away when Luke has made it so goddamn abundantly clear that he isn't interested?

Jack finally pulls open the door.

The way he's looking at me will give the wrong impression to whoever might be standing there, but like me, he's already pieced together who it is.

I stand tall and firm that I'm not doing anything wrong here.

"Ellie?" Luke says, his voice clouded with confusion. "What are you doing here? And why did it take so long to answer?"

My eyes meet his, and I'm about to tell him I only came here to tell his asshole brother to back off when Jack speaks first.

"She wanted to take me up on my offer, if you know what I mean." He elbows his brother in the ribs. "Not the first woman to enjoy the Dalton brothers, am I right?"

I gasp at his words. "That's not true," I hiss.

"Are you going to believe your brother or some broad you've known all of a few months at best?" Jack sneers.

Luke looks between the two of us. His eyes are a little bloodshot like he had another drink or four before he came up here, and instead of answering that question, he shakes his head. "Does it matter who I believe? You're going to tell the tale however you want it heard, and we're all supposed to just take you at your word."

"You didn't seem to have a problem with that when I was covering up *your* mistakes," Jack says, poised as ever while his brother seems to cower a bit.

Luke sighs. "I came here to try to have a conversation with you, but I don't know why I bother. I should know better by now." He seems...tired. Like this entire exchange has aged him a little while wearing him out completely. "Ellie, we'll talk tomorrow."

He turns to walk away, and I glare and hiss at Jack on my way by. I may not be done with this conversation with Jack, but the hell we'll talk tomorrow.

We'll talk tonight. Right the hell now.

I follow Luke down the hallway, and I'm sure Jack is laughing behind us as we move in silence toward the elevator.

I click the button to go up one floor to our room, and when the elevator arrives, I step on first. He doesn't move.

"I need some time to think. Can I trust that you're heading up to the room? Or do I need to worry that I'll find you in Jack's room again?"

I fume as the doors slide shut.

I didn't do anything wrong.

I go to our room and get ready for bed, and then I slide beneath the sheets and attempt to fall asleep.

When Luke finally gets back, it's close to two and anger simmers within me. I need to know where his head is at.

I'm not sleeping. How can I when each scene from tonight replays on a continuous loop in my mind? Luke's hunched shoulders. Jack's intense eyes. Kaylee's genuine friendliness. The parents' attitudes toward their kids. The confessions. The history. Savannah. The want and the pull. Jack's abs. Luke's weariness.

I'm confused, and I'm torn. On the one hand, there's the stable, kind man I've started building something with even though it's just a friendship.

And then there's Jack. He's a mystery. A wildcard. I know literally nothing about him, but he's been clear that he *is* interested in me.

I can't run to Jack, though. It's tempting, but I've somehow fallen for Luke. Even if he doesn't love me back, I can't do that to him...especially not after I learned about the history between the two of them and Savannah. I'd wager there's even more history between the two of them that I'm not privy to yet. How many other women have they *shared*? How many others got stuck in between them?

I don't want to be just another statistic on that pie chart, yet the attention from Jack tonight was some combination of warm and thrilling.

So when Luke finally walks into the room, my only real option is to pretend to be asleep. I'm not ready to face him along with everything that happened tonight...with everything that *could have* happened.

Besides, he waited a long time to come back up. He wanted me to be asleep. He's not ready to talk, either, and if he was, he'd wake me. Maybe. I guess I don't know him well enough to know the answer to that.

I hear the shower turn on. I wait for his side of the bed to dip down when he gets in...but it never does.

CHAPTER 3

When the light of dawn peeks through the curtains, he's still not in the bed we're supposed to be sharing. Of course I already knew this fact since I was busy tossing and turning all night.

I get up and find him asleep on the couch in the main living area. I try to be quiet so as not to wake him, but he shifts as I turn to go back into the bedroom.

"Morning," he says, his voice hoarse from sleep.

"Morning," I murmur. "Why'd you sleep out here?"

He sits up and winces a little, and I can't help but wonder what he did in the time between leaving him on the beach, seeing him in Jack's room, and when he finally came up to the room. He rubs his neck. "Figured you'd prefer it that way."

I sigh and sit on the coffee table in front of him. "It's just a lot to take in," I murmur.

"I know. And I'm sorry for the way I acted last night." He reaches over and takes one of my hands in his. "I care about you, Ellie. A lot."

I glance up to find sincere blue eyes locked on mine, and my heart wants so badly to believe him. My brain is still undecided.

"I don't know if we're doing the right thing," I say, withdrawing my hand from his grip. I don't want to. It's the last thing I want to do, in fact. But I can't hold his hand when I feel the way I do and when I know he feels the way he does.

It's too personal, too close, too intimate for two people who are nothing more than colleagues. "I don't want to be a pawn in the games you play with your family."

"You're not," he assures me. "That's not what this is, and the way I said it last night wasn't fair to you. Yes, I admit the reason I wanted to speed this up and do this in front of my family was to find some way to show up Jack. But Jack has nothing to do with the reasons we agreed to this in the first place."

"He hit on me." I knew I wouldn't be able to hide that tidbit from him. How does he do that to me? I'd like to say I'm nothing if not truthful...but clearly that's a lie since we're about to get married as a sham and I'm lying to pretty much everybody in the entire world except for Luke.

Oh, hell. I'm lying to him, too. I'm putting on the act like I'm not *totally* head over heels in love with him when I definitely am.

His face falls a little, but he quickly schools it back to indifferent. He *has* to have feelings about that, and I wish he'd show them. I wish he'd just fucking let me in.

"I ran into him when I left you on the beach," I say, giving him all the details he didn't ask for. "He came up behind me when I was waiting for the elevator."

"What did he say?" he asks, clasping his hands in front of him and leaning his elbows on his legs.

"He told me how you two like to share, and then he invited me up to his room."

"Fucking dick," he mutters. "And you went with him?"

"No." I shake my head. "He went up, and I followed on the next car, and I'm still not sure why. Maybe to tell him to back off. I was only there a minute when you came knocking."

"Telling him to back off isn't enough for him," he says. Then he lowers his voice and mutters, "Nothing is."

I stand. This suite is nearly a thousand square feet and it's not freaking big enough right now. "Well I'm sorry I didn't handle your brother to your liking when I had to get the hell away from you because you were so happy to let me know that you're just using me and you don't have real feelings for me."

He looks a little shocked at my outburst. I turn away from him and look out over the gorgeous view. I glance down to the spot where we're supposed to exchange vows in two days.

One thing he said last night is absolutely true: Hawaii is the perfect romantic backdrop for the wedding of my dreams to the man of my dreams.

But this is neither of those things. For one thing, the man of my dreams would want me back.

"He asked me why you're marrying me," I say, my eyes still out over the beach.

"What did you say?" His voice is a little distant behind me.

"I told him it's because you love me. He was adamant that you don't." I blow out a breath. "This is a bad idea, Luke. I just want to go home."

He's suddenly beside me. I didn't hear him stand or pad across the small distance to join me by the window. "I understand. I knew it was a bad idea from the start. I'll book your flight home. I'll be honest with my family. I'll figure out how to get Michelle off my back and keep Calvin happy without dragging you further into this mess. Actually, as my publicist, maybe you can help me figure out how."

I glance over at his profile as he looks out over the beach.

He's giving me a place to live and a job. He's become my best friend over the last few weeks—my *only* friend since I left everybody else behind in Chicago and Josh and Nicki are off doing their thing as newlyweds. He still wants me to work with him as his publicist.

He's my brother's best friend. I want to help him escape the demon women of his past and brand his image as the good guy the Aces can't live without.

And I love him.

All good reasons to marry him. But instead of saying any of that to him, instead of backtracking, I take the out he's offering. It seems like the only way to protect myself. "Thanks," I murmur. "And I'll start looking for my own place to live as soon as I'm back in Vegas." My heart twists as I think about Pepper and how much I'll miss her when I move out. Debbie, too, and my gorgeous purple and white office.

But most of all, I'll miss Luke.

Tears prick behind my eyes, but I blink them away.

He glances over at me. "You're welcome to stay as long as you need to."

I hold his gaze for just a beat. "I appreciate that," I say, and then I head to the shower, where I scald myself with heat and sob quietly into the water as I feel everything that was so close to my grasp slip away from me.

I only allow myself to feel that for as long as the shower lasts, though. I compose myself. I dry my hair. I apply some make-up. I get dressed.

Luke's sipping coffee in shorts and a flowery button-down shirt. He looks like the typical Hawaiian tourist, not the pro athlete he is. My heart twists again.

"Bad news," he says quietly. "The next direct flight out isn't until Sunday. If you don't mind a connecting flight, I can get you out later today."

"I don't know what I want," I admit. I want to leave *right now* before he has a chance to pin me with that gaze and change my mind. "Thanks for looking into it. I guess I'll just do Sunday." The words are out before I can stop them. *No! Take the one with a connection! Get out of here! Save yourself!*

The thoughts in my mind come too late.

"Do you want to come to brunch?" he asks. "We're supposed to meet my family in ten minutes. We can, uh, tell them the truth together if you want." He's holding in his emotions again, and it only serves to tell me I'm doing the right thing. I need to be with someone who's willing to let me in, and Luke has too many walls up that he's unwilling to tear down.

I'm sure he doesn't want his brother getting ahold of this news, and as his public relations manager, I want to be in control of the narrative...but the sooner we get it over with, the better.

"Okay," I say.

We head down to the restaurant. His parents, Kaylee, and Jack are already sitting at a table. Two open chairs wait for us at a round table, putting Luke next to Kaylee and me next to Jack.

Of course.

My heart races. Not only am I being forced to sit between these brothers who clearly have a sibling rivalry, but we're about to tell the truth about our fake relationship to his family.

My right knee bumps into Jack's as I sit, and he doesn't move his leg over. He's asserting his dominance or flirting or something, but to me it's just another example of what a cocky bastard he is. I glance over at him, and he smirks.

I want to slap that smirk off his face, and at the same time, my heart thumps loudly in my chest. I get it. I understand how he gets every-freaking-thing he wants in life. I can see how easily I'd succumb to his charms—maybe to hurt Luke because he's hurting me, too, or maybe because we'd have a lot of wicked hot fun together.

But I'm not meant to be a part of this family.

"Before we order, there's something I'd like to tell you all," Luke says after the good morning greetings are out of the way.

All eyes turn to Luke, including mine. So we're really doing this, right off the bat. We don't even get to enjoy brunch first, I guess. But this is a good thing. That way I don't have to wait and wonder when he's going to do it. I don't have to fake my way through another meal even though I'm faking far less than he is. I don't have to fight off Jack because once he has the proof that Luke isn't really in love with me, he'll lose interest.

"Actually, it's something we *both* need to confess," he says, glancing at me. I keep my eyes trained down on my ice water because I'm not sure I even *want* to see all the smug, self-righteous reactions on the faces gathered around this table.

Luke draws in a deep breath. "Ellie and I—"

"Sorry about the wait," the waitress says, interrupting what he was about to say when she bounds over to our table as if from out of nowhere. "What can I get for you?"

Luke hisses out a breath, and I glance over at him.

I shouldn't have.

I thought I was making the right decision by backing out, but when I see his clenched jaw working back and forth and his hitched up shoulders from the stress of simply eating a meal with these people and I combine those small things with the reasons why we were going to do this in the first place...I realize I'm back on board.

I can't let him call it off.

The way they treat him just isn't fair, and I want to be the person on his side. I want to stand up for him. Maybe it's because I love him, or maybe it's because he's paying me—but regardless, I *want* to do this.

Luke draws in a breath once the waitress skips away to put our order in. "Ellie and I have something to say." My eyes move to him, and he clenches his jaw for another beat. He opens his mouth to tell the truth...but I don't let him.

Not in front of Jack.

Not in front of his parents.

"We're getting married," I blurt before he can say anything more.

Luke's eyes meet mine. I see a question there, and I nod almost imperceptibly as I blink just once as if to will him to see that it's okay. The wedding is back on.

"We know that," Carol says with more than a touch of exasperated disapproval.

"No," I say, shaking my head with my eyes still locked on Luke's. "In two days. Here in Hawaii."

I glance at Kaylee, who looks nearly hopeful, and then at Carol and Tim, who both look disappointed. I can't force my head toward Jack just yet. I look back at Luke, and I see the question in his eyes melt into something else. Gratitude. Hope.

Heat.

"You're what?" Carol squawks.

Luke nods. "Getting married on Saturday." His voice holds a little bit of wonder, and I'm thankful for an actual show of emotion. Maybe there's hope yet for this guy. "To the love of my life." He leans in and presses a soft kiss to my lips, and damn if butterflies don't batter all the way around my stomach and my chest. "And we'd love to have you all there."

"Of course we'll be there," Kaylee sings. "And we're just thrilled to be welcoming you into the family, Ellie," she says to me with a big smile. "Right, Mom?" She elbows Carol.

"Of course," Carol mumbles.

"Well if that isn't just the happiest news I've heard all morning," Jack says, and his leg inches against mine again. "Congratulations, little brother." His voice drips with condescension.

I cross my leg at the knee away from Jack and toward Luke. I don't bother looking in Jack's direction. I lean in toward my fiancé and away from the man who seems like he just doesn't care about boundaries.

"We're very excited," I say.

Luke loops an arm around the back of my chair as a show of possession, and I lean further into him. It's not like it's difficult being close enough to smell his scent and feel his warmth, especially not in the presence of all these rather chilly people.

We suffer through small talk with Kaylee doing her best to lead the charge and Jack dominating most of the conversation. Luke is quiet to my left despite our announcement, though there's nothing out of the ordinary about that. I glance up at my future husband as Jack drones on about the Super Bowl again, and his eyes lock down on mine.

Thank you, he mouths to me, and I take the opportunity that's presented to me when I tip my chin up and give him a soft kiss that melts my insides to butter.

After all, we're about to be married. Surely betrothed couples kiss at the brunch table.

Once the interminable meal ends, Luke and I head back up to our room. As soon as the door clicks shut behind me, he lets out a long breath.

"Thank you," he says, turning to face me, and it's somehow reminiscent of our one-night stand when he looks at me the way he is as we stand near the door of a hotel room. "Why'd you change your mind?"

I press my lips together. "You deserve better than how they treat you."

"I don't deserve you," he says softly, his eyes flicking to my lips for a beat.

"You deserve the world, Luke." And by *the world*, I really mean *me*. I give him a sad smile. "The only one stopping you from having it is *you*."

He nods as he turns away from me, and he heads over toward the slider doors to look down over the beach. It seems to be where he does his best brooding. I move into place beside him.

"So we're really doing this?" he asks.

I nod. "We're really doing this."

A knock at the door pulls him from what was about to be a pretty intense brooding session. He turns to answer it, and I stay where I am, glad for the reprieve from his family.

It's a reprieve that's far too short as I hear Luke's voice. "What are you doing here?"

A male voice I don't know well enough yet responds. "We came to talk about this wedding."

CHAPTER 4

Luke's parents stand in the doorway, and eventually he opens the door a little wider to let them in. They both eye me warily before they help themselves to seats on the couch.

I don't move from my spot where I'm suddenly rooted to the floor.

Luke sits at the table, and he motions for me to sit, too. I hesitate but then I do it in a show of support.

"What do you want to talk about?" Luke asks.

Tim looks at Carol as if telling her to go ahead. She eyes him before she exhales a short breath.

"Why are you two doing this?" she asks.

"Why does anybody do it?" Luke counters.

"Some would say pregnancy," she says, raising an eyebrow in my direction.

"Oh come on, Mother," Luke says. "Do you really want to go there?"

"I'm not pregnant," I blurt. "That's not what this is about."

"I should hope not," Tim says. "Not when you've already got another woman pregnant." He shakes his head, his eyes down like his son is his life's biggest disappointment.

And *that* is why I'm doing this. I can't say that to them, obviously.

"So you two think I should be marrying Michelle, someone I can't stand and neither could you, simply because she's knocked up?"

Their silence speaks volumes.

Luke sighs. "I don't even have evidence that the child she's carrying is mine."

"You haven't asked for proof?" Carol asks, a tinge of surprise in her voice.

Luke shakes his head as his eyes move to the window. "It's complicated. I want to keep Calvin happy, but not at the expense of my own happiness."

"We didn't raise you that way," Tim says, and I have to admit...I'm curious what he means. They didn't raise Luke to think about his own happiness? He answers my question when he says, "We raised you to take responsibility for your actions."

"I am," Luke protests, but his words are weak and tired. I don't know him all that well, but he definitely strikes me as someone parents should be proud of. He's a good, kind, upstanding man, and getting someone pregnant doesn't diminish that in any way. "I've accepted that I'm going to be a father. I've taken action. I'll be attending her doctor's visits with her. I'm appeasing Calvin. I'm trying to do what's right."

"By marrying some girl you hardly know?" Carol asks, and then she pauses before she points a scary finger at her son. "Oh wait a minute," she says, her lips curling up shrewdly as if she's solved the puzzle. "Wait just one minute. That's what this is, isn't it?" She points that finger at me, and I feel like I'm going to throw up.

Luke closes his eyes and shakes his head. "I'm in love with Ellie. Not that it's any of your concern, really, but she's my best friend's little sister and I know her very well, thank you very much. We're walking down the aisle together out of love, and it's as simple as that."

Carol raises a brow at me. "And as for you, my dear? Getting a nice little compensation out of all this?" She circles her finger between her son and me.

I tip my chin up defiantly. I will *not* be intimidated by this woman. Except I totally am and I might pee myself as my next words come out of my mouth. "If by compensation you mean a husband I'm in love with, then yes."

Her lips thin into a pressed line, and my goodness she's scary.

"Well I think Carol has nailed it," Tim interjects. "I think you needed a way to keep Cal from going after you for impregnating his daughter, so you're marrying someone else to keep them at bay."

"That's not what this is." Luke is totally frustrated with having to defend our lie, and I get it. I'm frustrated, too. But I'm also starting to see that maybe his family knows him better than he realizes.

"Your story doesn't add up, son," Tim says. "You told us time and again after the Savannah fiasco you weren't getting married ever again, so why the sudden change of heart?"

"Love," Luke repeats. "I've never felt about *anyone* the way I feel about Ellie, and that's the honest truth. I was young and dumb when I married Savannah. I'm older now, and I like to think a little more seasoned and a whole lot wiser." He turns to me, his eyes locking on mine, and once again I'm struck that if this is all just for show, he's a damn good actor. "You don't just let someone like Ellie go because you made mistakes in your past. What we have has been powerful enough for me to see that I want to spend the rest of my life differently than how I've spent the first thirty-one years of it."

"We will be there, but I can't say that either one of us supports this," Tim says.

"I don't need you to support it, and I don't really care if you're there," Luke says, his voice full of venom. As it should be, really. His parents should support him even if they don't agree with him. My parents certainly would if the roles were reversed...except they don't even know I'm in Hawaii days away from getting married.

Tim stands. "A pleasure as always, son." His tone is full of sarcasm. He glances at his wife. "Ready?"

Carol stands, too. She studies the two of us for a beat, but her expression gives nothing away. As much as Luke wants to be nothing like these people, I suddenly see it very clearly. The way he schools himself to hold in his emotions—it's all there on Carol's face. She does it, too. Tim's the more emotive of the two, but even he really only seems to express anger and disappointment in Luke.

What the hell happened in this family that pushed them so far apart?

And, more importantly perhaps, what happened that made Jack the golden child while Luke was relegated to the outcast?

What the hell am I marrying into...and why am I still agreeing to it?

CHAPTER 5

Luke's hand is linked loosely in mine as we walk up the ramp to board the ship for the sunset dinner cruise Kaylee planned. I don't know if the rest of Luke's family is here just yet, but I can't say I'm looking forward to seeing them—especially not when I see how deeply they affect Luke.

We stroll around the rather large yacht and determine what we think will be the best spot to watch the sunset, and we run into the rest of the Daltons once we move into the dining room for cocktail hour. His parents and his siblings are already seated at a table, and two open seats await Luke and me.

I suck in a breath just as I notice my future husband doing the same. I glance over at him, and we lock eyes. I let out a soft chuckle, and he does, too. Funny how we're both bracing ourselves for whatever this evening has to offer. To say I'm dreading another meal with this family is an understatement.

"Nice of you to join us," Carol says when we take a seat.

"I didn't realize we were late," Luke asks with a touch of exasperation that's nearly borderline implying they should be glad we showed up at all.

Carol purses her lips.

"This mai tai is fantastic," Kaylee says, jumping in as usual to try to salvage what's going on. This whole routine is getting a little old, to be honest.

I glance at Luke. "I could use a drink," I say.

"I don't know if I'll make it through this meal without one." Luke smirks and stands.

"There's the Luke we all know. Substances to numb, right?" Jack says under his breath.

Luke glares at him before he strides away. I have to practically run in my heels to catch up to him as we make our way toward the bar.

"What was that all about?" I ask.

He rolls his eyes. "Just Jack being Jack."

"Substances to numb?" I ask, repeating what Jack said.

Luke stops in his trek to the bar and glances around like he's making sure nobody will overhear us. "I was hurt early in my career and I took injections before games to help numb the pain."

My brows pinch together. "Like painkillers?"

He shrugs. "Toradol. It's basically strong ibuprofen."

"That doesn't sound so bad." And the truth is...it doesn't. Ibuprofen is common after injuries, right? But if it's not so bad...then why did he glance around us before his admission to make sure nobody was listening? Maybe there's more to it, or maybe he just wants this conversation to be on the down low.

"It's not," he says, moving his feet again as we head at a slower pace toward the bar. "Jack has taken it, too. Everybody does. Some guys take it before every game. I only took it when I needed it."

I'm not sure I care for the *everybody does it* kind of argument. It reminds me too much of when I was a teenager and my mom asked whether I'd jump off a bridge if everybody else was doing it when I simply had asked if I could go to a concert with my friends.

For the record, I was the only one out of my group of friends who wasn't allowed to go. Nothing bad even happened, so that's one bridge I could've jumped off of.

"So why'd he call you out on it just now?" I ask.

"Because he's Jack." His tone is exasperated again, and I don't quite like that he's directing his attitude toward me. It was funnier when it was toward his mother.

I order Kaylee's recommendation of a mai tai because, well, when you're in Hawaii, you drink mai tais. Luke orders a beer for himself, and then we head back to our table with his family and I think I'm going to need four or five more of these to get through this dinner.

"So tell us how you two met," Kaylee says to me. "All Luke said was that you're Josh Nolan's sister."

I launch into the story we made up together even though the real one is actually a whole lot more interesting.

Luke's arm is around the back of my chair, and he's turned in toward me as I talk, interjecting little details here and there, and the story actually sounds real. We've told it enough times now that it sure as shit should.

"She couldn't resist my charm, and I've never been happier in my life," Luke says at the end, and he leans forward and presses a soft, chaste kiss to my lips.

I melt.

I. Freaking. Melt.

I wish that kiss was real. I wish his words were real. I wish *all of this* was real.

I try not to gloat as he pulls away. He smiles at me, and the adoration in his eyes looks so genuine that even I am falling for it at this point.

But it's all an act, I remind myself.

We eat, and both Luke and I are fairly quiet as Tim dominates the direction of the dinner chatter with stories of

Jack's heroics when it comes to the field. It's all a bit of a bore, if I'm being honest. I already wasn't super thrilled with football talk, and when it's focused on someone other than Luke, I lose interest fast. But I guess I'd rather sit idly by than the alternative of defending our decision to get married even one more time to the Dalton family.

We head outside after dinner to watch the sun as the ocean swallows it up, and the scenery is beautiful. Luke's arm is around my shoulders, and his lips brush my temple, and I squeeze my eyes shut as conflicting emotions crash into me. On the one hand, I relish being so close to him and feeling the love coming from him. On the other...disappointment lances through every part of my being that it's just a show to him. He's just playing the part for his family's benefit.

And when we're not with his family, the show appears to be over. He's quiet again. He retreats back into himself.

The day after tomorrow, we're getting married. These days should be filled with love and excitement, but an impending sense of dread washes over me. I just have this feeling that something is going to go wrong at the wedding.

"I'm going to go for a walk if you'd like to join me," I say once we're back at the hotel room.

"Thanks for the offer. Have a nice walk," he says.

Whatever. I head down to the beach all alone. I could sit up in the stifling room with him as he broods, or I could walk the beach and try to soak in more of Hawaii while I'm here.

We're not even to the halfway point of this trip. I should've taken him up on the offer to leave with a connecting flight. I might not even have had to sit through brunch this morning. Instead, I'd be on my way home and out of this mess.

Even as I think it, though, I'm reminded that *home* is really just Luke's house. There's no escape.

Fair GAME

He's paying me well for the publicity. He quadrupled my rate when I signed the contract with the lawyer with the stipulations for our arrangement. He *said* the pay was for my public relations work, but we both know it's a legal way for him to pay me to marry him, and right now that thought makes me feel hollow.

I've taken a bunch of photos of him and with him while we've been here. I should be set with content for the next year. I've posted on his behalf a few times, though nothing indicating we're in Hawaii, and I've gotten excellent feedback, more follows for him, and a handful of sponsorship requests that I've forwarded to his agent.

I sit in a lounge chair by the pool for a few minutes and scroll through my spank bank—I mean *professional photographs*—of Luke. I pick one out and post it along with a question to engage his fans.

I click off my phone with the intention of heading toward the beach for a solo walk where I can lose myself in my thoughts. But before I get the chance to stand, a voice stops me.

"What are you doing out here all by yourself?"

I glance up and find Jack's penetrating navy eyes focused down on me.

He's all alone, too.

And suddenly I feel like I'm very much in danger.

CHAPTER 6

"Oh, uh, hey Jack," I stutter. "Luke was tired."

"So it's just the two of us, all alone. At least we're in public this time." He raises his brows then laughs at his own joke.

I'm not laughing.

He slides onto the lounge chair beside mine, and my heart races. I don't like being alone with him—not because he poses any sort of physical threat, but because I still don't understand the relationship between Luke and him. I'm nervous I'll say the wrong thing.

I'm nervous he'll get me to agree to something I shouldn't agree to.

I glance over at him. He's relaxed on the chair, eyes trained up toward the sky. I wonder how often he gives in and relaxes like this. He doesn't seem much like the type of man who even knows *how* to relax.

"I'm not sure what you're getting at," I say quietly, "but I'd like to make it clear that I'm in love with your brother."

He sits up and turns to face me. His eyes glow in the soft blue light bouncing up at us from the pool, reminding me of the night I met Luke and he first kissed me by a pool.

"I'm not getting at anything, Ellie." The way he says my name makes it sound so...sexual. "Just trying to be friendly as I get to know my future sister-in-law."

I keep my eyes focused on the pool. "That's all I'll ever be to you."

He huffs out a laugh. "Oh come on. We're all well aware that this is just some PR stunt. Aren't you handling his publicity? At least he could've picked a better cover up."

"It's not some PR stunt," I lie, doing my best to defend Luke, but let's be real here. I'm a bad liar.

I think about changing the subject and confronting him about the little Michelle bomb he dropped on me, but he asks a question before I get the chance to bring it up.

"If it's not for PR, then why don't *you* have anyone here to witness this shindig?"

Dammit. He's smarter than I thought. "Because we decided last-minute to do this here. We want to get married before training camp, and we agreed Hawaii was the place to do it."

"Okay, I'll play along. But for the record, you could have me if you want me," he says.

I choke, and he lets out another laugh. I don't even know what to say to that. Do I want him? Maybe. Sure. Of course. He's sex on legs, for God's sake. But he's Luke's evil brother, and I'd never do that to Luke. I couldn't.

I feel like maybe this is my opening to bring up Michelle. He mentioned her in passing, and I need to know if it's true or if he was just pressing my buttons. As a beat of silence passes between us, I can't quite figure out how to broach the topic. *Did you really sleep with Michelle? Any chance you knocked her up and not Luke? Are you the ticket to helping us get her the hell out of our lives?*

I just feel like I'm not quite lucky enough for that last one to come true.

"So why are you really marrying my brother?" he asks before I get the chance to bring her up.

"Because I love him." At least I don't have to lie about that.

"You've known him all of five minutes. You don't know him well enough to love him. And if you did..." he trails off, but his words are a clear indication that I wouldn't love him if

I knew him. I feel my hackles rise with the sudden dire need to protect Luke at all costs from whatever Jack thinks he can do or say.

"That's not true," I say. "I know him very well after all the time we've spent together."

He raises a brow and lowers his voice. There's nobody within hearing distance, but I notice how both Jack and Luke ensure their privacy when they say things they don't want anyone else to know. It feels oddly good to be in the inner circle of people on the receiving end of those lowered voices. "So you know about the shit Savannah holds over both of us? Did he tell you about that? Did he tell you about what we did to cover up *his* mistakes? Did he tell you how damning the evidence she has is? How it could fuck up both our careers and how we both pay her to keep her mouth shut?"

"Of course he did," I snap. It's another lie, but it's not like I trust Jack to sit here and tell me the truth. He's just trying to make waves. He's trying to catch me in something and I won't sit here and take it. I stand. "I'm going to bed," I say.

It's not what I had planned. I wanted to go for a walk on the beach. I wanted some time to myself away from anyone who has the last name *Dalton*. Instead, I'm either stuck sitting with Jack as he does everything he can to squeeze the truth out of me or sitting in silence in the room with Luke.

I think I need to go with silence.

Not because it's what I want, but it's why I'm here. It's what I'm being paid to do.

As I walk up to our room, I realize I've now been confronted by Carol, Tim, and Jack—twice—about marrying into this family. I guess three down, just Kaylee to go.

But first...I need some answers.

Luke's watching football when I walk in. He barely even looks in my direction.

Some way to greet your fiancée.

"What does Savannah have on you?" I ask.

He stares at the screen a few beats before he clicks the power off and turns toward me. "What?"

"Jack mentioned Savannah holds something over the two of you. He confronted me just now asking if I know everything, and he made some pretty strong insinuations that you two covered something up that could come back to hurt you both now. So I'll ask you again, what does she have on you?"

Luke sighs and glances away from me, and it's that very moment I realize I don't know him. At all. I don't know if glancing away means he's about to come up with a lie. I don't know if Savannah really does have something on them that she's covering up. I'm marrying this guy, and I don't know truth from lies. I don't know what's real and what's fake.

"Jack's just trying to get under your skin," he says.

"Well it's working," I spit. "And you're under my skin, too. I fucking hate all of this. And by the way, Jack thinks this wedding is fake, among many reasons because there's no one sitting on *my* side of the aisle."

"Then we'll pay someone to act like your friend."

I press my lips together and nod slowly. "Right. Good solution. Throw money at the problem." I huff out a sigh. "I'm going to bed. Goodnight."

I'm not tired, but lying in bed seems like it beats talking to Luke or potentially running into Jack again.

CHAPTER 7

My inbox has another Luke Dalton email alert when I wake up—alone again—in the morning.

I click the link, and it's a picture from last night on the boat. His lips are brushing my temple. Our body language says it all. I'm happy to be there beside him. I'm leaning into his kiss, and his arm is around my waist, and if I didn't know better, I'd think I'm looking at a couple very much in love.

I glance through the article. It doesn't mention specifically where we are in Hawaii or the fact that Luke and I are getting married. It's just some hot trash letting everyone know that we sure are cozy on a boat together.

I take my phone out to the main room of our suite where I'm sure Luke's asleep on the couch. My intent is to wake him with the latest article, but he's already up, his eyes trained on his phone. He glances up at me when I walk in, and I flash my screen at him with a smirk. "You see the latest?"

"Good morning to you, too," he mutters. He sits up and winces, and then he stretches his neck like it's stiff. "And yes, I saw the photo."

"Someone's watching," I say, not really feeling all that bad for him that he has a stiff neck. It was his choice to sleep on the couch for another night. The bed is plenty damn big.

He blows out a breath. "Someone's always watching, Ellie. It's a part of this life and it's only a fraction of why I enjoy my privacy. My popularity index is rising with your hunger traps and I'm not sure I like it."

"Thirst traps!" I scream at him. "They're *thirst traps* and you're real fucking welcome for building your platform to make you indispensable to the Aces. You're real fucking welcome for doing everything I can to help you with your problems. You're real fucking welcome—" I stop yelling at him—screaming like a banshee, really—when I hear a knock at the door.

My eyes widen.

How thin are these hotel walls?

Did anybody hear what I was just screaming?

I glance at the door, and then I look back at him. I just rolled out of bed. I'm not in the mood for guests. "You can handle that," I hiss, and then I head to the bathroom to take a long, hot shower. Once I'm dressed, I find Luke on our balcony, brooding once again as he looks over our view. "Who was at the door?"

He keeps his eyes trained on the ocean in front of him. "Housekeeping. They wanted to clean our room." He glances up at me. "Kaylee texted me a while ago and asked if we wanted to meet for breakfast."

"Sure," I say. "And I'm sorry I exploded at you before. This is just...it's all just a lot, Luke."

He presses his lips together. "I know. And thank you for all you're doing." He clears his throat. "Give me fifteen minutes," he says, and it's his turn for the shower.

That's it. No apology for his words. No hugging it out. No reassurance that we're doing the right thing.

My phone starts ringing as I'm sitting on the balcony waiting for him, and when I glance at the screen, my heart squeezes.

Fair **GAME**

Very few people actually call my phone anymore. If anything, they text...but my best friend is someone I talk to on a daily basis. When she's in the country, anyway.

And I've missed her. I've been going through this alone, and the one time I thought about calling her on her honeymoon to get some advice was the one time I followed Jack to his room and was tempted to make a poor decision that came from a place of anger and pain.

"Hey, Nicki," I answer. My voice is filled with exhaustion even though I'm trying to fake enthusiasm. I don't particularly want to have this conversation, but I'm tired of feeling completely isolated.

"I'm back from Fiji ready to tell you all the stories and imagine my surprise when I saw a headline that you're in freaking Hawaii with Luke and his entire family!"

Shit. I need to be careful not to reveal that we're here to get married. "He invited me to come along on his family's annual trip."

"To show off his fiancée?" she presses.

"Something like that."

"And how's Hawaii? We thought about going there instead of Fiji. Tell me every detail."

I laugh. "We're heading to breakfast in a few minutes but it's great. We'll find time to chat soon. How was Fiji?"

She launches into some story that I'm half-listening to about how my brother kept getting stopped at the airport to sign autographs. I stare down at the beach. I've looked at all this a hundred different ways, but hearing Nicki's voice feels like home, and it's reminding me once again what Jack said last night. He's right. There's nobody here for me.

Luke steps onto the balcony, and I interrupt Nicki. "I'm so sorry, babe, but we're heading out now. I'll call you later, okay?"

45

"Of course. Love you!"

We hang up. "Sorry. That was Nicki." A flash of alarm passes over his face, but before he can say anything, I say, "I didn't mention anything about getting married."

He nods. "Okay. You ready to eat?"

I stand. "Here's to hoping it's just you, me, and Kaylee."

He chuckles, and we both step back inside. When he closes the glass slider, he stops. I turn back to see what's holding him up, and his eyes lock on mine. "In case I haven't told you recently, thank you. You're an incredible woman, and I appreciate you and all you're doing for me."

I press my lips into a thin smile. "Thank you for all you're doing for me, too."

We leave it at that, and we head down to breakfast. My hope that it would be just the three of us is shattered the second I spot Jack sitting beside Kaylee.

"Good morning," Luke says brightly, reminding me once again of his stellar acting skills as his hand tightens over mine.

"Morning," Jack murmurs, his eyes on me before they slide down to where Luke clutches my hand.

I feel scrutinized with the way he's looking at me. I force my hand more firmly into Luke's, but then we're done walking and we're at the table and it's just awkward for a beat as we let go and sit.

"This is our annual sibling breakfast," Kaylee explains to me. "We do one without Mom and Dad so we can chat about whatever we want without parental judgment."

"She's not a sibling," Jack points out, his eyes on me.

Heat creeps up my neck.

"Close enough," Kaylee and Luke say at the same time, and then they both laugh.

Kaylee smiles at me. "You're getting married tomorrow. We'll count you in as part of the family."

"I won't until tomorrow," Jack says, his eyes edging over to Luke.

"Don't be an asshole," Luke says to his brother.

Jack lifts a shoulder. "Until the vows are spoken, she's fair game."

I glance over at Luke, who looks like he's about to pop a vein in his head.

She's fair game.

That seems to be Jack's motto.

Kaylee clears her throat. "Jack, be a decent human being," she says. She looks at me. "This is just such a repeat of the past. These two have a, um, *colorful* history."

"So I've heard," I murmur. "I'm happy to leave you three to it." I move to stand, but Luke's hand finds my thigh. He puts some pressure there, forcing me back to my seat.

"Stay. Please. Don't let Jack push you away." He leans over and presses his lips to my cheek, and I get a whiff of his freshly showered scent and *God* do I want him a little more every single second.

"Sorry," Jack says, holding up his hands in what might be the most insincere apology ever. "It's just not fair to invite someone to a sibling breakfast when she isn't actually a sibling."

"You want to talk about what's *fair*?" Luke demands.

"You think it was fair to marry my fucking ex-girlfriend?" Jack spits back.

And that's it. That's the root of the problem between these two men.

Jack never forgave Luke for being with Savannah even though he gave them his blessing. And now Jack will spend seemingly every waking moment making Luke pay for that.

"Guys, stop. Lower your voices. People are looking," Kaylee says.

"You're only getting married to somehow come out looking better than me," Jack says, completely ignoring his sister, "but it's the opposite. You look like a mess. We all know you just want to take some of Mom and Dad's attention off me. You're always so desperate for their approval, but it's so obvious to everyone that all this," he pauses to wave his hand between Luke and me, "is just a charade. Some PR stunt. I just can't figure out *why*, but rest assured, I'm working on it."

My heart thumps in my chest. Is this where we drop the act?

Is Luke really so desperate for his parents' approval that he'd go to these particular lengths? I guess he's going to these lengths for his team owner's approval. I wonder for a half-second what that relationship is like. Is Calvin a pseudo-father to him? Another person to try to impress?

"Fuck you, Jack," Luke says.

"Stop it!" Kaylee yells, and silence falls over our little table. She lowers her voice. "Stop it. You know people are always listening. We don't need you two blowing up the media by fighting about personal matters in public."

Luke's eyes move to his water glass, his mouth shut in his own way of conceding to his sister's good point, but Jack is not to be stopped.

"Just admit it," he says quietly.

"The only thing I'll admit is that I have fallen in love with Ellie." His voice is soft, but there's still ice in his tone.

When I glance over at him, his eyes are on me. They're tender and kind, adoring and loving, if I didn't know the truth, I'd believe him. I'm part of the lie and I very nearly believe his sincerity right now.

He leans forward and presses a gentle kiss to my lips.

"I love him, too," I say. My words are my truth.

"You two are the cutest," Kaylee says, clearly approving.

"What a fucking joke," Jack mutters. He stands and tosses his napkin on the table. "I'm out." He stalks out of the restaurant, which is fine by me. I'd rather eat this meal without him here anyway, and I'd bet money Luke would, too.

And all this goes down before we even order our freaking pancakes.

CHAPTER 8

"Why is he so bent on this idea that we're faking it?" I ask, if nothing else to break the intense, awkward silence that falls over us after Jack stalks out.

"That's just Jack," Kaylee says, like that excuses his rude behavior. "He gets an idea in his head and doesn't stop until he gets his way. And in this case, proving he's right means getting his way, so he's going to pick and pull at every thread and push the two of you to the edge to prove his point. For what it's worth, I believe you."

A surge of guilt pulses through me. She believes us, but she probably shouldn't. Jack doesn't, and I wish he would. What a mess.

"Thank you," I say softly. Luke tosses an arm around my shoulders and squeezes me to him. He presses his lips gently to my temple in a public display of affection for his sister's benefit, and I can't help but wonder if he feels the same surge of guilt that I do.

Breakfast is decidedly pleasant once Jack leaves. Luke and Kaylee catch up, and I sit quietly observing as Luke tends to deflect questions back to her. He's friendly as he makes conversation, but he leaves personal details almost completely out of the equation.

Except for Pepper. He lights up when he talks about that adorable pup.

Kaylee is animated and she's the kind of over-sharer who gives every detail about her life—so, in essence, the complete opposite of her brother.

I learn she recently ended a three-month relationship because they had vastly different visions of the future. She wants a litter of children and dogs and he didn't. I learn that Kaylee is in her last year of college and she's majoring in education. She wants to be a middle school teacher—the hardest group of youngsters to teach, I'd imagine, but growing up with two brothers her elders by at least a decade seems to have given her a thick skin. I learn that she and her roommate are in the middle of a fight because her roommate finished her box of cereal…Lucky Charms, naturally.

Oh to be twenty-one again.

"What's on today's agenda?" Luke asks.

Kaylee smiles then makes the motion to zip her lips.

My brows dip. "What's this about?"

Kaylee laughs. "Today is excursion day!" She's positively gleeful as she says it. "Whenever we do these family trips, whoever picked the location gets to plan two excursions. The dinner cruise was one and I have a mid-morning and afternoon surprise planned for today."

Oh yay. So after the awkward breakfast encounter with Jack where he wrote me off as unimportant to this family, I'm so blessed and lucky to get to spend more time with him today. Carol and Tim, too, who gave us that awkward wedding pep talk about how we shouldn't do it. I really just can't wait to spend more time with these people.

Luke's arm is still around my shoulder, and his fingers dig into my flesh for a beat as more than likely the same thoughts run through his mind.

"Do we need to bring anything or wear something special?" I ask.

Fair **GAME**

She shakes her head. "What you're wearing is fine. It's just a fun, relaxing little thing today."

A fun, relaxing little thing. With Luke's family. I'm not sure those two ideas can comfortably coexist.

We head right for the lobby when we're done eating, and the rest of Luke's family is already waiting there for the three of us—Jack included.

"Good morning, everyone," Kaylee says. Everyone exchanges morning greetings and then we stare at Kaylee awkwardly as she taps some things on her phone. I still can't imagine ever feeling awkward around my own family. Even Kaylee must feel it, but she blows past it because she's trying to build memories. Clearly she wants all this to be normal, but it's just...not.

She finally looks up with a smile. I can't tell if it's forced or not. I can't tell if any of these people should've gone into acting instead of athletics or if they actually do have real emotions they can express. "Our car will be here in a few minutes."

We all pile into the luxury SUV Uber that Kaylee called and we're on our way to the surprise location. We only drive for maybe ten or fifteen minutes as Kaylee murmurs about the beauty of the scenery and the rest of us remain quiet when the driver pulls into a parking lot for a beach.

A beach much like the one where we're staying.

Why, exactly, did we need to drive fifteen minutes to get to another beach?

The answer is made abundantly clear as I spot several large, beastly animals tied up to stalls near a shack. It would be a lovely picture of horses on the beach...if I liked horses.

I don't.

They terrify me.

I pray with all my might that the horses are *not* the excursion she has planned, but we all already know that of course it is' since this is my life and it couldn't possibly be any other way.

Kaylee opens the door and we all tumble out of the vehicle, and then she claps her hands together. "Horseback riding on the beach!"

My heart races so fast that my chest actually hurts.

My first instinct is to flee. I look around for a place to run away, somewhere to hide until this is all over, but I don't see one except the little shack where we need to go to get set up for our adventure.

I stand frozen to the spot, my eyes focused on those damn horses as all the color drains from my cheeks.

What the hell am I going to do? I can't just bolt. This is a *family* excursion. I'm going to be a part of this family, no matter how temporary that may be. It's part of the job description to go out and bond with them, isn't it?

I just never thought I'd be bonding over *horses*.

Equinophobia. That's my thing. Fear of horses. And that's the only thing I can think of as I ball my trembling hands into fists in some attempt to feel something other than fear as my knuckles turn white.

"Uh, Kay?" Luke says.

She looks up at him. "Yeah?"

"Ellie doesn't care for horses," he says, and my cheeks that had blanched just a second ago now start to burn with mortification.

It's not that I don't *care* for them.

I'm fucking terrified of them.

"Of course she doesn't," Carol mutters, and if I wasn't all wrapped up in my own thoughts about these damn horses, I might be offended by that—I might even question why she'd say that.

But I can't. Instead, all I can do is stare at the animals from where I stand. Why, exactly, do people ride horses? They're animals. They're wild. They're not meant for us.

I inhale a large breath and hold it for a beat.

I can do this. I won't be trampled. They're just gentle animals. They won't hurt me. They won't buck me off their backs.

I clear my throat as I repeat those mantras that I certainly don't believe on any level. I'm not trying to be difficult in front of his family. I'm just genuinely panicked here.

"It's fine," I say, a tremor to my voice. I clear my throat to try to get rid of the shakiness and press my lips into a small smile.

Luke's brows dip. "It's *fine?*" he says.

I shrug and nod. If these people can all act their way through anything, if they can all wear these facades and masks and hide their real emotions...well I can, too. "Yeah." I say it with a nonchalance I don't feel on any level. "Let's do this. It'll be fun." Random phrases tumble out of my mouth, but I don't really mean them.

"You sure?" Kaylee asks, her brows pinched, and at the same time, Luke says, "You don't have to do this."

"It's fine," I repeat, my fists still clenched as my nails bite into my palms.

Luke tries to grab for my hand as we all turn toward the shack to check in for our ride, and I physically have to make myself unclench my hands to grab his. I think I grasp his a little harder than I mean to.

He leans into me. "Are you okay?"

I keep my eyes focused forward, somehow landing on the back of Jack's head, and I nod. "Fine."

He squeezes my hand in solidarity, and then we're at the shack and it feels an awful lot like there's no turning back now.

Why do I continually feel that way around this family over and over again?

Jed, the man who runs this whole operation, leads us out to the beach. He points to six of the eight horses in their stalls. "We have Clementine, Dale, Sugar, Domino, Fiona, and Scout. Pick your horse and we'll get you all saddled up."

He gives a few more instructions, and then Luke asks, "Which one is the gentlest?"

"Sugar. She's a sweetheart. Aren't you, girl?" Jed says, rubbing a palm on her muzzle.

She doesn't look like a sweetheart. She's brown with a little white on her and isn't he scared she's going to bite his hand off when he pats her nose like that? She's a huge beast of an animal easily ten times my size, not some gentle creature.

"Take Sugar, Ellie," Luke says to me.

I blink and nod as I try to reconcile the fact that I'm getting on this thing with the fear that permeates my entire being. It starts in my heart and with every beat, it pulses out into my veins. The pounding synchronizes in my head, ba-boom, ba-boom, ba-boom, every beat setting me further and further on edge.

I spot Jack as his eyes edge over to me, a sly smile curling his lips.

Why do I get the premonition like something bad is going to happen that has nothing to do with the horse?

Everyone else mounts their horses except for Luke, who's still standing beside me. I'm standing a few feet away from Sugar as I try to force myself to get on. Luke grabs my hand and squeezes it.

"You sure you're okay with this?"

I draw in a deep breath and exhale, and then I just do it without answering. I brace one foot on the stirrup and toss my other leg over, and magically I'm on top of a horse. For a second I'm stunned that I made it this far, and then I grab onto the little knobby thing sticking up—I think Jed called it a *horn*—since I already feel like I'm going to fall off.

What if I fall off and the horse tramples me?

It's my biggest fear, and one I really didn't think I'd ever have to face. Certainly not today when I woke up this morning.

I try to draw in a deep breath, but it doesn't seem like I can fill my lungs enough. I exhale short, sharp breaths.

"Ellie and I are going to skip this one," Luke says, patting Dale on the side.

I can't help it when I glance over at his family to gauge the reactions to that. Carol tuts disapprovingly and Kaylee's eyes are full of disappointment.

"It's fine, Luke," I grit out. "Get on your horse."

I guess if anything, I have the option of sitting out by myself, but if this is going to somehow help Luke bond with his family, then I'm going to suck it up and just do it.

Jed unties the horses from their stalls and leads the pack of us down toward the water. We're moving slowly, which I'm thankful for, but somehow Jack ended up next to me—not Luke. Luke is behind me.

I feel Jack's eyes on me, but I can't look over at him. I'm focused forward because if I tear my eyes away from the spot between Sugar's ears for even a second, I might fall off.

"You seem to really enjoy horses," Jack says, and I hate that I can picture his smirk at just the mere sound of his voice.

"Let's just enjoy the ride in silence," I suggest.

"Oh, but where would the fun be in that?" He laughs, and I wonder if Luke can hear our conversation or if he's too far back to catch it over the clopping sound of hooves hitting wet sand. "It's just such a romantic ride on the beach. Just think of it. You ride this horse now, and the invitation to ride the stallion is still open if you'd like to stop by later."

My jaw drops in shock, though it really shouldn't. He's been hitting on me since practically the moment we met, and I'm pretty sure he does it just to get a rise out of me—and to piss off his brother.

I still don't look over at him. "Thanks, but I'm busy. With your *brother*."

"You know that old saying about being hung like a horse..."

I gasp. "Oh my God, Jack!" I'm about to finish my shrieking with something about how inappropriate that was, but it would appear that gasps and screeches spook poor old gentle Sugar.

I suppose it might've helped if I would've listened to Jed over the rushing fear between my ears earlier as he told us what to do if our horse gets spooked, but instead I was too focused on my fear. As Sugar's front two legs shoot up into the air and she spins to change direction, my brain computes that horses flee when they're afraid.

I'm afraid, too.

Beyond afraid. I'm freaking the fuck out. I don't know what the hell I'm supposed to do as my horse runs along the beach and away from the Daltons at what feels to be lightning speed. I simply grasp onto her neck for dear life and close my eyes, praying that Jed will be able to catch up to us and save me.

Sugar is moving so fast that the saddle is starting to slip around to the side. Maybe she puffed herself out when the saddle went on to give herself more room or something, but it's not snug around her and I'm clenching my thighs to try to keep balance as the saddle starts to move. My body is still on it, and I cling to her neck as my life flashes before my eyes.

I'm not on the beach anymore. I'm not riding the horse. I think I might've blacked out. I don't hear anything except the rushing in my ears. My eyes are squeezed shut tight as fear permeates every atom of my being and pieces of my life flash before me.

I had a good childhood. Josh and I fought, sure, but we were always close. My parents did what they could to give us memories to last a lifetime. Family vacations, barbecues with neighbors, memorable birthday parties, Christmas mornings with so many presents we had to take breaks unwrapping them. And even my adulthood has been pretty good. I've had my share of failed relationships, of assholes, of frogs dressed as princes until I saw what was really on the inside.

There's the good and the bad, and if I come out on the other end of this alive, I'm going to have to take a good, long look at my life.

I thought I was on the right track here. I thought I'd somehow met my Prince Charming and I was heading toward a happy ending. As I flail on this horse that I'm no longer riding (at least in my mind, I'm not, because I would never ride a horse, and instead, I'm just being taken for a joyride on a really scary rollercoaster), I finally realize that I need to come to terms with what's really going on.

Should I really be wasting an entire year of my life on someone who doesn't love me?

Or is it really wasting it if it has the potential to be everything I think it could be?

CHAPTER 9

I finally force my eyes open when the wind whipping around me seems to slow. I realize I'm still riding a horse on the beach with the Dalton family.

That's when I stifle a scream.

Screaming will only spook the horse further, but then I see Luke on a horse beside mine. I see Jed as he grabs the horse's tether on my other side.

I'm saved, and a lump clogs my throat.

Everything comes back into focus, and then Sugar stops completely.

I jump down off this bitch and run up the beach as fast as my legs will carry me.

I collapse onto the sand once I'm far enough away from the horses and I lose all control as the rushing terror starts to melt into something resembling gratitude.

I'm still alive.

I'm off that horse.

Luke was right there to save me.

Like a goddamn Prince Charming galloping in on his steed.

I burst into sobs.

Ugly, gross, wet sobs.

He is a fucking prince. Okay? He just is.

These tears aren't from what just happened. Okay, they're not *entirely* from what just happened. The horse galloped, and I was slipping off, and I got scared.

But I'm marrying the guy who seems to be my prince every single way I look at it except for the one way that really matters in a marriage.

And that's a whole lot more terrifying than some stupid horse.

I wrap my arms around my legs and tuck my head down into the hole to cry in peace. I'm certain the entire Dalton family is watching. Maybe they're laughing, maybe not. Jack is, probably. Luke might not be.

And that's when I feel his arms come around me. He holds me for a beat, and his hands move in soothing circles around my back. "Are you okay, Ellie?" Luke asks softly, and he presses his lips to the top of my head.

"I'm okay," I sob into my little dark hole. "I'm so sorry."

"Hey, hey," he says quietly. "There's nothing to be sorry for. You're okay. I've got you." He keeps rubbing those circles, and see what I mean? That whole thing about being torn between whether this has real potential or I'm wasting a year of my life. It doesn't feel very wasteful when his arms are around me.

"She's fine," he yells, maybe to his family or maybe to Jed. I'm not sure since my head is still down in my little hole. "Go on ahead."

He lets me cry a few beats as he keeps rubbing my back and whispering soothing phrases. "Look at me," he eventually commands softly.

I lift my chin out of my hole, and he thumbs away my tears as his navy eyes bore into mine. His sunglasses are flipped up on his forehead, and concern and apprehension shade his view as he gazes at me.

"You're okay. I'm right here with you, and you will never, ever have to ride a horse ever again. Not for me. Not for my family. Not for anybody. Do you hear me?"

I nod but can't seem to form words around the huge lump in my throat. The horse could've hurt me. But so could Luke, and it's not like I can just hop down and run away from him like I did Sugar.

"Thank you for trying," he says. "You didn't have to do that."

I sniffle and try to draw in a deep breath, but the air comes in short little spasms as I attempt to calm down. I'm definitely letting him think the tears are from the whole Sugar incident, not from this situation I find myself in with my husband-to-be.

I wipe my eyes with the bottom of my shirt and take a swipe under my nose, too, all the while trying to calm my breathing so I can inhale deeply enough to feel satisfied again.

"Can't wait to see what else Kaylee has planned," Luke mutters, and I can't help when a small giggle bursts out of me. I'm riding some emotional highs right now, and I'm not sure if I've ever had sobs turn to laughter at the snap of a finger before, but his words strike me as incredibly funny in the moment.

His eyes lift to mine again, and he chuckles when he sees the fear in my wild eyes replaced with just a hint of merriment.

"What happened out there?" he asks. He hasn't moved from his spot kneeling in front of me.

"Jack said some really inappropriate things to me and I sort of shrieked and I think I scared the horse," I say.

Luke shakes his head and grits his teeth. "I'll fucking kill him."

I set a hand on his arm as I'm finally able to draw in a breath. I don't need family violence over this. "It's fine," I say. "I'm fine. Everything's fine."

"What did he say to you?"

I stare at him for a beat, and then I realize I have zero reason to protect Jack in this. "An invitation to ride the stallion who's hung like a horse," I admit.

"Jesus Christ." Luke closes his eyes a beat, and when he opens them, they're stormy with anger. "I can't believe him. I'm so sorry."

Does it really matter? It's not like you want me.

I can't bring myself to say those words.

It's not like I'd take Jack up on his offer anyway.

"Just forget about it," I say.

My gaze falls across the beach. The rest of the Daltons continue on their adventure, with Jed leading the pack. Our horses are tethered together and near the stalls again. We're safe, and they're all far away and heading even further from us.

Thank God.

And so that's why when Luke leans in and nuzzles my nose with his, a dart of surprise pings my chest.

His family isn't watching. They're riding horses, judging the girl who they assume is overly dramatic and did something to make the horse run away when really it was Jack's fault.

This isn't for their benefit.

His warmth and his proximity and this moment...it all feels like it's just for us.

His lips are centimeters from mine, and my body lights up this close to him. His heat washes over me, and every detail of our single night together rushes back to me. His tongue in my mouth. On my body. His hands gliding across my skin. His fingers pushing into me. Fingertips clawing the glass of the window.

I freeze as I pray he'll kiss me.

Instead, with his lips centimeters from mine, he speaks so softly I almost miss his words. His voice is tortured as he says,

"You deserve so much more than him. More than me. I wish I could give you that."

You can.

"You can." The words slip from my lips before I can stop them. I don't want to stop them. I want him to see that we're made for each other. Why can't he just see that?

His lips brush mine as if he just can't help himself, and then he backs away. "I can't." He stands, and he pulls me up with him, breaking the moment we just shared. He doesn't even give me a second to regain my composure or to brush off that kiss that made my knees weak. "I'm glad you're okay."

"Me, too," I admit. "But no more horses. Like ever again. Okay?"

He chuckles. "Deal. I saw a brewery up on the boardwalk. Should we go grab something stiff?"

I raise a brow at his choice of words. I'd *love* to grab something stiff.

Oh great, now I'm starting to think like Jack.

I push that thought quickly away, but Luke laughs at the look on my face anyway as he grabs my hand and we move up the beach toward the boardwalk.

Kaylee's whole idea here was to bond her family, but instead…it feels an awful lot like this horseback riding fiasco has only brough Luke and me closer together.

CHAPTER 10

"Double vodka seven," I order.

I realize we're at a brewery and the traditional order might include the beer that's actually brewed here, but even though I'm breathing normally again, my nerves are still on high alert. I'm not quite over nearly falling off a horse for the second time in my life.

And then there was that kiss and his words.

I sigh.

"I'll try your IPA," Luke says, and the bartender slinks away to make our drinks while Luke taps out a text. "Just letting Kaylee know we came up here."

I roll my eyes. "Can't wait for them to join us." My voice is full of sarcasm, and he chuckles.

"This might be a strange time to say this, but I'm really glad you're here," he says. He sets his phone down on the bar.

"You are?" I can't hide the surprise in my voice.

He drums the bar a little with his fingertips. "I don't know how this vacation might've gone if I didn't have you here by my side."

My eyes feel a little misty at that. "Really?"

He lifts a shoulder and keeps his gaze trained down on the bar top. "You see how they are. It's worse when it's just me and them. At least they're civil in front of other people. Most of the time." He shakes his head. "My parents, anyway. Not Jack, apparently."

I reach over and squeeze his hand, and instead of responding to any of that, I throw out the question I need the answer to. "Why are you so convinced that you're wrong for me?"

He's quiet a while, and I give him time to think about that since I popped that question out of nowhere. The bartender drops off our drinks, but I'm not letting Luke out of answering just because we're distracted by drinks.

He holds up his glass to mine. I clink and we each take a sip.

Okay, *sip* is a bit of an understatement. I gulp down half mine and Luke does the same.

He blows out a breath. "I'm thirty-one. I don't want another real marriage because I've already tried it and it didn't work for me. I don't want to go through that devastation again." He rubs the back of his neck. "I should know what I want out of my future by now, but I don't. I'll be sharing a child with someone I can't stand, and I don't really know if I want more kids than that. I've got a past, I don't know what my future will look like, and it's all just a lot to burden someone with."

"I get all that, Luke. I do. But *everyone* has a past. Everyone has baggage."

He presses his lips together but doesn't answer.

"You won't even give this a shot," I press. "And you're saying it's because you don't want to burden me?" I shake my head. "You haven't even thought about whether I'm willing and able to shoulder those burdens. That's what marriage is, Luke. It's a partnership."

He stares straight ahead. "You deserve more than I can give you." His voice is nearly robotic, like he's saying the words he's trained himself to say. There's no emotion there, but there rarely is with this guy. He gulps down the second half of his beer.

Fair GAME

I nod and sip my drink just to give my mouth something to do other than tear into him because I'm about to unload all my thoughts on that. He doesn't know that. He's given me *everything* I could possibly ask for in the short time I've known him.

Everything except himself.

He's given me friendship. Shelter. A job. Food. He takes care of me. He gets off his horse so he can make sure I'm okay and he rubs my back when I fall.

I feel it, and I *know* it can't just be me.

Every sign points to the fact that he cares about me as more than just a friend...every sign except the only one that matters.

His affirmation.

I drain my vodka. "I deserve happiness," I finally say. "We all do." *And I think you can give me that.*

His drink is empty, too. He motions the bartender over. "And in the long run, I don't know if I can give you that."

I drop the subject before I start to sound desperate...if it's not too late already. I'm not asking for forever. I'm just asking him to give this a real shot because I think it could be something incredible for us both.

"So what does the future look like for Luke Dalton? You'll play football as long as you can, and then..." I trail off as I wait for him to fill in the blank. We've sort of covered this topic already, but he didn't really have a definitive answer.

"It's bad luck to talk about what comes next," he says. "I'll worry about it when I'm there. Despite my age and the statistics, I don't feel like I'm anywhere near the end of my career at this point."

"I didn't peg you as superstitious," I admit.

He chuckles. "I have three rules, Ellie. I eat Lucky Charms and blueberry waffles with peanut butter on them for breakfast on game day. I listen to the same playlist each week to get in the right pregame headspace. And I don't talk about what happens after my days on the field come to an end."

I laugh. "What's on the playlist?"

"That's confidential," he says with a wink and a twinkle in his eyes. "Top secret."

"I'll find out," I promise.

"Good luck," he scoffs, clearly teasing me. "I have two hundred playlists. You'll never get it."

"I only have to be wrong a hundred ninety-nine times, babe."

"Assuming, of course, that you have access to said lists," he points out.

I take a sip of my fresh drink. "All right. Until you confirm otherwise, I will just be over here believing that your game day playlist is a power mix of hits from Celine Dion, Adele, and Whitney Houston."

"Don't forget Mariah Carey," he says, and then he covers his mouth in jest like he just gave away a secret.

I raise a brow, and his eyes continue to twinkle, and it's just another moment that I fall in deeper. I'm going to live to regret this, but there's just no turning back at this point.

"You really won't tell me what's on it?" I ask—mostly because now I *need* to know. He can't dangle something so silly in front of me and expect me not to dig until I get my answers.

He shrugs. "Nope."

"Celine it is, then," I tease.

He narrows his eyes at me. "Hey, you could do a lot worse than Celine Dion."

We're both still laughing when the entire Dalton clan walks in through the front doors of the brewery, and suddenly all the merriment and laughter is sucked right out of the room. I feel it physically drain out of me, replaced instead with a mix of anxiety and irritation...especially when my eyes meet those of a smirking Jack.

CHAPTER 11

"There she is," Jack says as the entire family approaches the bar where we sit. "The horse whisperer."

"Shut the hell up, Jack," Luke hisses.

"Boys, boys, let's give it a rest," Carol says, her voice tired as if she's been telling them the same thing for the last thirty years. She glances at me before settling a disapproving gaze on Luke. "You couldn't grab a table for the rest of us?"

My brows arch and my eyes widen at her words.

She doesn't ask me whether I'm okay.

She doesn't tell us how much fun they had.

Not even a fucking *hello*...but a complaint about our choice of where we decided to sit when we came here alone while the rest of them continued on their adventure right after I almost died.

"I didn't realize you'd all be joining us," Luke says. He glances around and nods to an open table—of which there are plenty in here, for what it's worth.

"Didn't you get my text back?" Kaylee asks, and Luke shakes his head as we pick up our drinks and follow Carol toward the table.

Kaylee falls into step beside me. "I'm so sorry, Ellie. I had no idea you didn't like horses or I never would've planned that for everybody. You okay?"

I nod and press my lips together. What happened was terrifying, but I give the dramatics a bit of a break. "I'm fine."

"You're a mind-reader, Lu Lu," Kaylee says. "This was activity number two. Lunch at a brewery. You know, since I'm of legal age now and all that jazz."

We take our seats at the table and a waitress comes right over with menus. We've been sitting less than thirty seconds and I already miss my alone time with Luke. We were laughing, and he was opening up even if he was saying things I didn't want to hear, and we were pulling closer to one another. And then his family shows up, and it's like he regresses. He's a turtle retracting back into his shell, and it'll take another near accident or an act of God or something to get him to come out again.

I hate what they do to him, and I just want to get away from them.

Especially Jack, who keeps looking at me from across the table. I feel his eyes on me, and I try to ignore it. But every time I glance up, our eyes lock.

He always gets what he wants, right? And right now, he wants to prove that what we're doing is nothing more than a sham. The funny thing is that he *is* right. But he thinks that he can just keep hitting on me and eventually I'll give in.

I won't.

"So what happened out there?" Kaylee asks.

I lift a shoulder. "I guess my horse got a little spooked or whatever and he just took off the other way."

"The way you were holding on, I thought you were practicing for the Kentucky Derby." Jack smirks again.

"Knock it off, Jack," Luke says, his volume rising.

"It's fine," I say. "I can take his teasing." Because I can. That's a way to show affection. It's part of being in most families, right?

Jack holds up both palms innocently.

"This whole thing is your fault," Luke says to him.

Kaylee, Carol, and Tim just watch the tennis match as it unfolds. I sit uncomfortably as I wait for Luke to drop the truth bombs in front of his parents.

Jack's brows arch. "My fault?" he repeats. "How, exactly?"

"You know exactly how," Luke hisses, pointing a finger at him. "You need to stop hitting on my future wife. We're getting married *tomorrow* and she's not interested."

"Why don't you let her tell me that?" he asks, never losing his cool despite the rare show of emotion from his brother.

"I have," I say, finding my voice despite the extreme awkwardness of this situation. "I'd appreciate it if you stopped."

"And speaking of our wedding, our rehearsal is tonight," Luke says.

Carol purses her lips. "So there's nothing we can do to stop this?"

I meet Jack's eyes across the table, and he looks...confident. Arrogant.

I have a sinking suspicion that he has a plan, and the thought scares me almost as much as that damn horse.

Luke's arm moves around my shoulders. "We're going through with the wedding." His voice is firm and holds no space for argument.

"Our little conversation didn't have any impact on you at all?" she asks.

Oh, it had an impact all right.

Luke shrugs with nonchalance, but his fingers digging into the flesh of my shoulder tell a bit of a different story than what he's projecting to his family. "It did have an impact, actually. It made me see how very much I need Ellie in my life."

He leans over and presses a kiss to my temple, and something tells me he's not just tossing out a jab with those words. I think he actually means them. But what, exactly, he means *by* them is a different story entirely.

"You know we all think this is a mistake, Luke," Tim says. "It's too fast." He avoids looking at me, and in that moment, the truth finally strikes me.

I suppose I sort of get it. Tim is trying to watch out for his son—his professional athlete son with a healthy bank account. He doesn't know we've signed papers that keep Luke's assets perfectly safe. In his own twisted way, he's trying to show he cares. Carol, too, I guess. And maybe even Jack—maybe he thinks that he can lure me away and prove I'm not in this for the right reasons.

They have a funny way of going about it, but maybe it's the only way they know how, particularly since Luke is so closed off even with them.

"Leave them alone," Kaylee interjects softly. "Can't we just enjoy our lunch and talk about all this later? Can we stop fighting for two seconds and just enjoy a little time together as a family? This should be an occasion of joy. Luke has found the love of his life, and they're getting married. Let's celebrate that instead of forcing our opinions on them."

I look at her gratefully, and another dart of guilt pierces my guts. I wish we could let Kaylee in on the truth, but it's just too risky.

"Thank you, Kay," Luke says softly.

A beat of awkward silence falls over the table, as if nobody really knows what to say if they're not fighting.

"So tell us what we missed," I finally say. "How was the horseback riding?"

Kaylee launches into their tales of horses splashing through the surf. The four of them are laughing as they retell their adventure that I'm only half-listening to. Instead, I'm studying them. All of them. They moved from the tense argument to laughter on the turn of a dime, and meanwhile I'm over here still trying to play catch up.

And my future husband seems to be, too, as he stares down at his beer in silence.

Gone is my laughing, fun Luke from a few moments ago, replaced with this brooding man. I just wish I knew how to get the other Luke back.

CHAPTER 12

Luke and I have a quick meeting with Alana, our wedding coordinator, in the front lobby regarding details for tonight's rehearsal when we get back from lunch. We're still sitting in the comfy chairs in the lobby when it happens. We watch as a taxi pulls up in front of the hotel, and then two figures get out of it.

Familiar figures. A man and a woman.

It takes my brain a second to catch up with what my eyes are seeing.

"Oh my God!" I screech once it all registers, and then I pop up out of my chair as I run toward the hotel entrance. I toss my arms around my brother's neck. "What are you guys doing here?"

"Hey, Sis," Josh says, and I move to Nicki for the next hug. She's a golden tan from her honeymoon, her blonde hair streaked with even more highlights than usual, and she wears a bright smile.

"Oh my God, it's the bride!" she gushes, and I can't help my giggle as I recall saying that to her not so long ago when I arrived in Vegas for their nuptials. I squeeze her, grateful suddenly to have someone here for me...someone who can sit on my side of the aisle.

I thought having Luke here was enough. He *should* be enough, and he has been...in those few times when he has actually allowed me in.

But now that I've met the family, I realize I need an entire army on my side to get through tonight and tomorrow.

"Didn't I just talk with you on the phone this morning?" I ask her.

She giggles. "We had just boarded our plane when I called you. I was testing the waters."

"What are you doing here?" I ask Nicki since my brother didn't answer the same question. I glance over at Luke. His eyes are twinkling at me. He had to have been the one who clued them into where we are and what we're doing here.

But why would he do that?

As I recall, it was his idea for the two of us to travel to Hawaii before these two got back from Fiji just so they didn't have the chance to try to stop the wedding.

"Josh came to talk you two out of it," she admits softly in my ear. "I came to stand beside my best friend as she marries my husband's best friend. I'm here to support you in whatever way you need support."

Tears spring to my eyes. I needed them both here more than I realized.

"Why don't you two get checked in and meet us in our room so we can talk?" Luke suggests, and the newlyweds head toward the check-in desk while Luke and I go to our room.

We're quiet on the elevator ride since we're not alone, but once the door closes us into privacy in our room, I spring the only question in my mind on him. "Did you do this?"

He shrugs then smirks, and that smirk is so devilishly delicious that it just makes me want to jump his hot bones. "I *may* have had something to do with it."

I toss my arms around his neck. "Thank you," I say, and then I untangle myself before I get carried away. "But why?"

He flops onto the couch where he's been sleeping the last few nights, and I slide into a chair at the little table across from the couch.

"I know this has been hard on you," he admits. "It wasn't just Jack pointing out that you don't have anyone on your side of the aisle. It's the fact that you don't have anyone here *at all*. I know I can be closed off, and that's something I'm working on. I have a hard time letting people in because of how I've been burned in the past even though I'm starting to realize how much I can trust you. I guess I just wanted you to know that even if I don't always show it, I do care about you."

"So you called in the very people we were trying to avoid finding out about this because we thought they'd try to stop us?" I ask, the confusion clear in my tone.

"I told them the truth. They're the only people in the world who know apart from you, me, and my lawyer." He glances out the window before his eyes return to me. "They can try to stop it if they want. But this is between you and me. Do you still want to go through with it?"

I blow out a long breath, my gaze out the window now. "I don't know why, exactly, but yeah. I do."

"I do, too."

My eyes return to him, and he lets off a soft chuckle.

"That almost sounded like our vows," he says.

"You better give me a little more romance than that. At least if you want your family to buy it."

He's still laughing when he opens the door a few beats later. My brother and my best friend are standing there, and I still can't quite believe they're really here.

"So what the hell is this?" Josh asks, walking into the room.

I haven't moved from my spot at the table, and Nicki takes the chair next to me.

Luke blows out a breath and falls back into his spot on the couch. "It was supposed to just be a fake engagement, but your sister said she'd really marry me to shut up Michelle."

"And Todd," I remind him, and Luke nods.

"And Calvin," Luke says.

"Probably Jack, too. Pretty much everyone, really," I admit as I see from yet another angle how this is the only way to help Luke with his public image.

"Calvin?" Josh asks.

"He confronted me about the headline with the pregnancy scandal at the Beating Hunger in Vegas Charity Ball," Luke says. "He's pissed that I got Michelle pregnant and I'm not marrying her. He told me I need to get my priorities in line, and then he reamed me a new one in his office a few days later."

Josh shakes his head. "Oh man," he laments.

"Where *are* your priorities?" Nicki asks, and I'm sort of surprised she's the one jumping in with that question.

"I want to protect Ellie. I want to ensure my child is taken care of. And I want to fucking play football." He ticks off those items, seemingly in no particular order...but I can't help noting that I was first in that list, and his public image is nowhere on it at all.

"My sister better be first," Josh says, catching onto the same thing I did.

Luke sighs. "I'm sorry I dragged you into this," he says to me, and part of me wonders whether he really means it or if he's saying it for my brother's benefit.

"It's not like I put up some huge fight," I say. "Part of what you hired me for was to fix your image, right? Really, that should be on your list of priorities, too."

"But it's a stupid reason to get married," Josh says. "You two can't do this."

"We're doing it, and we invited you here to support us," Luke says firmly.

Josh seems angry. He looks from Luke to me and back again as he tries to form words to reply to that.

"Josh, it's okay," I say softly. "We've been back and forth over this a hundred times. Believe me. But we're both okay with it. We've both signed papers to protect ourselves. We're going in with eyes wide open. Luke has been so kind to help me, and I want to help him, too."

"I knew asking if she could stay with you was a mistake," Josh mutters.

"It wasn't a mistake," I say softly. "This is something we both want. We both benefit from it."

"You don't get married because you're benefiting from it. You get married because you love the other person," Josh says. He glances at Nicki, who's been uncharacteristically quiet during this whole thing. The way he looks at her tells me they're having some silent conversation that only the two of them are privy to.

"There are lots of reasons to get married," I say. "Maybe this isn't the traditional way, but we've talked out every angle. We've had his family trying to stop us for the last few days, so it would be great to feel like we have someone on our side here."

"Are you going to tell Mom and Dad?" Josh asks.

I clear my throat. "To be perfectly honest, I haven't really thought that far ahead."

"Eventually they'll find out, right?" Josh asks. "Once the media gets wind of it, it'll be everywhere. Don't you want to get ahead of that and tell them before they find out from someone else?"

"As soon as it's official, I'll call them," I say. I'm *really* not looking forward to that call.

"Don't you think they'll be upset they weren't invited?" Josh asks.

My eyes edge over to my soon-to-be-husband, who's awfully quiet during this exchange. I'm reminded of the magnitude of what we're doing, but that doesn't change the fact that I still want to go through with it anyway.

"We'll just tell them the truth," Luke says.

"You sure about that?" I ask.

Luke shrugs. "I trust you and your family implicitly." He motions toward my brother. "Obviously, or else I wouldn't have called in these two and filled them in on the truth."

I trust you and your family implicitly.

How come his actions and his words don't match up? He keeps giving off the vibes like he doesn't care, but then he does things that absolutely show that he does.

I guess he's just trying to make this situation more comfortable for me. He cares about me as a friend. He cares about me as the little sister of his best friend.

But despite inviting Josh and Nicki here and little things here and there that make me start to think otherwise, his words have been pretty solidly consistent in letting me know that's where it ends.

Nicki and Josh glance at each other, and then Nicki clears her throat. "Ellie, can we talk somewhere privately?"

I nod and stand. "Bedroom?"

"Oh yeah," Luke says lewdly. "To the bedroom."

"Come on, dude," Josh whines. "That's my wife and my *sister.*"

I giggle as Nicki follows me to the bedroom. I close the door behind her.

Before I even get the chance to turn around, she says flatly, "You're in love with him."

"What?" I ask, my hand flying to my chest in surprise.

She rolls her eyes. "It's so obvious, Ellie. Just admit it."

My brows dip. "What are you talking about? This is nothing more than a business arrangement. I'm in charge of his branding, and he's paying me to work as his publicist. That's it. His public image needs some help, so I'm doing what he's paying me to do." I'm babbling, and it's *totally* giving me away. I'm a bad liar, and Nicki knows me far too well. I need to shut it before she sees right through me.

"Then why do you look at him with hearts in your eyes?" She folds her arms across her chest. "Why are you doing this? Do you think he's the answer and you're finally going to get your happy ending with your Prince Charming by trapping some guy into marriage?"

That's sort of the thing about best friends, isn't it? They know everything about you, and they're here to point out the things you're pretending like you can't see. I appreciate what she's doing, and I appreciate that she's trying to be here for me in any way she can, but at the same time, I'm so damn tired of fighting everybody off.

"What happened to supporting me in whatever way you can?" I demand.

She sighs. "I don't want you to get hurt." She sits on the edge of the bed, and I collapse next to her.

"Too late," I admit.

"What's really going on here?" she asks. She lies back, too, and we're both staring up at the ceiling.

I sigh. "I have a confession."

"Yes?" she says, drawing out the word in a sing-song tone.

"I'm totally in love with him." I toss my arm over my eyes.

"Yeah, no shit. So what are you going to do about it?"

"There's more," I say. I might as well get it all off my chest at this point.

"More?"

I nod even with my arm still covering my eyes. "You can't tell Josh."

She tugs my arm, and when I glance over at her, she's lying on her side, leaning on her elbow as her hand props up her head. "I tell Josh everything, so if you want this to be a secret, don't tell me. But please tell me regardless of that."

Eventually he's going to find out anyway, right? I decide to rip off the bandage. "Remember my one night stand the night of your bachelorette party?" I move to mirror her position.

Her brows pinch together as it hasn't quite clicked yet. "Yeah..."

"It was Luke."

Her eyes widen. "It was *Luke*?"

I nod.

"How did you not know who he was?"

"You know I don't pay any attention to football. Although if I knew the players looked like him, maybe I would." I waggle my eyebrows playfully even though I know this is a serious conversation.

"He didn't know who you were, either?" she asks.

"I guess not. Josh probably just referred to me as his sister, not by name. It's not like he showed off pictures of me to his friends. Quite the opposite, in fact. It sounds like he warned them all off me."

"He didn't," Nicki breathes.

"Oh, he did," I confirm. I move so I'm lying on my back again, staring up at the ceiling again as I recite the story. "And Luke and I..." I trail off and sigh as that night comes back to me.

"Luke and you..." she repeats, prodding me into telling her the dirty details.

"We were strangers who met at the bar in a club even though neither of us is a clubber. We had one amazing, incredible, hot as fire, molten, steamy, unforgettably orgasmic night together, and then we parted ways. I snapped a selfie of the two of us so I could brag to you the next morning, but you were busy doing bride stuff so I held off. And actually, before I even got to your house, I ran into him at Starbucks, overheard him bragging about his conquest, which was me, and we had a little confrontation before I spilled all my coffee everywhere and it was the most embarrassing moment of my life so I told him I wanted to just pretend like I never saw him that morning."

"He was *bragging* about you?"

I nod. "Yeah. To Josh."

Nicki stifles a laugh. "Oh my God, wait until he finds out."

"To be fair, my plan was to brag about it to you, too."

"As I recall, you did. For a minute. But your parents were there making brunch." She laughs, but I'm failing to see what's so funny about my life.

Ah, who am I kidding? It's a freaking comedy.

"So then what?" she asks.

"Then Josh introduced him as his best man at the rehearsal dinner and I about fainted and then we became roommates and it's all backwards and so messed up and I went and totally fell in love with him. He's a goddamn prince."

"Oh, Ellie," she says softly. "How does he feel about you?"

I'm quiet for a beat, and then I answer honestly. "I have no idea. He's so closed off with his feelings that it's impossible to tell, but I keep thinking that he *does* feel something for me. It's just that he's been very clear I'm off-limits, whether it's because of some agreement he has with my brother or some misguided attempt at chivalry or something."

"I'll find out."

I sit up, and I shake my head as I stare down at her. "No," I say. "I don't want you getting involved."

"Too late," she says simply, and I'm a little terrified of the can of worms that I may have just opened.

CHAPTER 13

I stare at the video on my phone that was posted less than thirty minutes ago.

"Oh-em-gee, do I have some *piping* hot tea to spill today," Billy Peters says. The photo I saw this morning in my inbox alert flashes across the screen. It feels like a decade has passed since that moment. I nearly got killed by a horse, had some laughs with Luke at a brewery, faced off against his family for the umpteenth time since they arrived on the islands, and ran into my brother and sister-in-law.

What a day.

And it's not even over yet.

"Here we have Luke Dalton and fiancée Ellie Nolan, sister of the Vegas Aces star wide receiver Josh Nolan." As he talks, a heart forms around our faces. "But get this nugget. Jack Freaking Dalton, Luke's older, more successful, and arguably hotter brother, is there, too. Wait...is he hotter?"

The screen flashes to a side-by-side of the brothers, and no one can deny they share a lot of genes. Both ridiculously handsome, both with chiseled features, both with dark blue eyes. "I can't decide. Sound off in the comments. Anyway, they're all in Hawaii right now, and football star Nolan and his new bride just showed up, too. Any guesses why those closest to this hot couple would be flocking to the islands?"

He pauses, as if waiting for someone to scream an answer at whatever device they're watching this shitshow on. "It's not to get lei-ed." Billy winks. "That's right, peeps. Lukey Luke is there to *marry* his best friend's little sister. But his not-so-believing big brother was overheard questioning the legitimacy of this union. The words *charade* and PR *stunt* were used when Jack accused Luke of getting married for nefarious reasons, including the accusation that he's simply seeking their parents' approval. And believe it or not, there's more! Luke used to be married to...wait for it..." he pauses for a few beats, and then he says, "Jack's ex-girlfriend!" His mouth drops open with over-the-top dramatics. "I'll be digging into that today, so be sure to stay tuned for all the latest." He snaps his fingers and moves onto the next celebrity victim in his line of fire.

"Shit," I mutter.

"I'm so sorry to be the one to show you this," Kaylee says.

I shake my head. "No, don't be. You were the one telling them not to talk about it in public."

She nods as she presses her lips into a thin smile. "This was why."

"Luke!" I yell. We have a half hour before our rehearsal is set to begin. My hair and make-up are done, and I'm moments away from getting out of my sweats and into the dress and heels I brought along for the occasion.

He appears in the bathroom doorway. He hasn't even started getting ready yet. I roll my eyes and shake my head as I think to myself, *men*.

"Yes, my love?" he asks, and I swoon at the term of endearment for a beat before I get to the point of why I called him in here.

"Did you see the Billy Peters video?" I ask, and he nods.

"The guy's a douchebag. I don't really care what he says."

"That's fine, but we need to hurry up and get ready. We need some pictures of the two of us to post as soon as possible to shut down rumors regardless of whether you care about

Billy Peters. Super romantic stuff that shows how much you love me, 'kay?"

He chuckles. "Whatever you need, babe."

Kaylee sighs dreamily. "Gosh, you two. If people would just *see* you two together, they'd know it was real. They wouldn't even question it."

I press my lips into a thin smile at Luke as she heads out of the bathroom and toward the living room of our suite.

They wouldn't even question it.

I'm a *part* of it and I question it daily.

"How can you not care what he said?" I ask when it's just Luke and me.

He shrugs nonchalantly. "Shit like this gets posted all the time. You learn to tune it out."

Will I learn that, though? It sure doesn't feel like it. And it's not just that. I'm worried about Luke. I'm worried about Calvin getting hold of this information. How will he treat Luke at work if he knows this is just some stunt—and will he piece it together that it's a stunt for *his benefit*? He owns a freaking football team. It's not like he cruised into that position without some shred of intelligence.

We need to keep it quiet, and we need to make sure it's believable. Luke's job might be at stake if his boss allows personal vendettas to get in the way of his professional life, and after Luke's "reaming," I'm not so sure of Calvin's intentions.

Luke runs a comb through his hair, brushes his teeth, and gets dressed, and he's ready to go in under five minutes. He zips the back of the navy dress I chose, and I slip on my heels.

He studies me for a beat, and I cower a bit under his intense scrutiny. "You're stunning," he finally says.

So are you.

I wrinkle my nose instead of saying that. "Really?"

He chuckles. "And adorably modest, too." He taps my nose, and I giggle.

We head down to the beach with Kaylee, who is waiting for us in the lobby.

We're first. Alana isn't even here yet, and the sun is just starting its descent into the water.

The lighting is *perfect*.

"Kaylee, would you mind taking some shots?" I ask. I whip out my phone and pass it over.

"Of course not," she says, and she sets to work. Luke turns on the show. He kisses me. He holds me. He embraces me. His fingertips skate down my bicep. His arm comes around my shoulders. It may be a show, but it *feels* real. And all this against the backdrop of swaying palm trees and a nearly setting sun on the island of Maui as the sky boasts pinks and reds and golds.

I'm scrolling through the photos, admiring Kaylee's handiwork as well as what an attractive couple we make with Luke's arm tossed casually around my shoulders.

Luke and Kaylee are admiring the sunset beside me when I hear Nicki's voice. "Oh my God, there's the bride!"

I giggle, select one of my favorite images of the two of us with a simple ring emoji in the text, and click the post button before I shut off the screen.

Jack walks in with Carol and Tim a minute later, and Alana strides in last to begin our rehearsal.

"Ellie and Luke, the two of you will stand here," she says. "And since we don't have a maid of honor or best man, it'll just be—"

"Change of plans," Luke interrupts. "My best friend just got back from his honeymoon in time to attend, so if he's up for it, I'd love for him to be my best man."

We all turn and look at Josh, who looks uncomfortable. But rather than blow our cover, he simply says, "Yes, of course. I'd be honored."

Everyone's eyes turn toward me. "And I'd love for Nicki to be my matron of honor," I say.

She squeals before she rushes over and hugs me, and I take that as a yes.

Alana runs quickly through the ceremony, explains where the guests will stand, answers all our questions, of which there are few since this all seems pretty straightforward, and then we're released to dinner.

It was quick and painless, and to my extreme surprise, Jack stayed in his lane.

In less than twenty-four hours, I will be Mrs. Luke Dalton.

I feel a little weak in the knees at the thought, and I'm just crossing my fingers (and toes for extra luck) that everything goes according to plan between now and then.

But this is *my* life. Of course it won't.

CHAPTER 14

"It's not the bachelorette party I envisioned throwing for you since we were teenagers, but it'll have to do," Nicki says. Our feet are submerged in our own little footie-bathtubs as we wait for our pedicures to begin at the hotel spa after dinner.

Josh whisked Luke away for one last night out as bachelors, and Nicki brought me here.

"Room for one more?" Kaylee asks.

"Of course!" I say, perhaps a bit too enthusiastically as I pray and cross every finger and toe I have that Carol isn't also on the guest list for this little shindig...and that Jack isn't on the guest list for Luke's party. I highly doubt we'd be that lucky on both fronts, though.

Do I really want Kaylee here? No, not really. I'd love to chat unfiltered with my best friend, but it looks like that's not what the universe has in store for me tonight.

I lean back in the chair and work the remote for the massage elements built into the back. Some ball back there rolls up and down my back, and I feel more relaxed than I've felt in weeks.

Probably since before I met Luke Dalton.

My life has tumbled into a chaotic mess since the night we first met by chance at the bar. I almost miss the good old days when I was obsessed with glitter stickers and my bullet journal and had a crush on a boy I worked with who ended up not being very prince-like *or* very charming...you know, like a couple months ago.

"What are we doing after the pedicures?" Kaylee asks.

Nicki shrugs. "Club?"

I wrinkle my nose. "The last time I went to one..." I start to say, but then I trail off. The last time I went to one, I met Luke, and we had a one-night stand, and now I'm marrying him. Nicki knows this after our conversation yesterday, but Kaylee does not, and we don't need Kaylee finding out when we're this close to pulling this wedding off.

"Ooh, what happened?" Kaylee asks.

"I drank way too much," I lamely finish, and Nicki laughs.

"*Way* too much," she agrees, and I shoot her a glare. She turns to Kaylee. "It was my bachelorette party not so long ago. We partied in Vegas and this one could hardly handle her liquor."

Kaylee giggles. "Was Luke there?"

"Oh, Luke was there," Nicki says, and my eyes are bugging out of my head as I fear that Nicki's about to give away our secrets. She doesn't, though. She's a better actress than me. Instead, she says, "Come on, Ellie. It's your last night as a single woman. Let's live it up and have some fun."

I huff out a *fine* since she seems hellbent on this idea. Once my nails and toes are a very lovely, albeit virginal, bridal white, and they've dried the appropriate amount of time under the ultraviolet lights, we head upstairs to change.

An hour later, we're standing at the bar and I glance around the club. Blue and purple lights bounce off the walls, and there's even a few disco balls spaced evenly around the ceiling to make the lights glitter as they move. It's a typical club except for one thing: nobody on the dance floor is actually holding a drink.

The bartender approaches us, and Nicki orders a mai tai for each of us.

Just what I need. Rum.

We all turn to move toward the dance floor when the bartender calls our attention. "No drinks on the floor," he says, nodding toward the swell of people dancing.

My brows dip down. "We can't dance and drink?"

He shrugs. "Maui laws."

Nicki, Kaylee, and I all glance at each other, and then we shrug and tip back our first drink of the night. As I chug, I pray it doesn't make my face too puffy for my wedding day tomorrow, my mother's words from the day after Nicki's bachelorette party fresh in my mind about whether I'd had too much to drink because of how I looked.

Once we finish our drinks, we move to the dance floor. I feel positively ancient next to the young twenty-somethings (like Kaylee) dancing up a storm to songs I'm no longer familiar with, but I put in my best effort.

I'm two or three—possibly four—drinks deep when someone sidles up next to me at the bar while I'm waiting to order another round.

"Hey good lookin'," a deep voice says close to my ear. "You come here often?"

I chuckle.

"The last time I saw a sexy lady waiting by herself for a drink at the bar," the deep voice continues, "she was looking for someone to fuck just for one night."

I shiver at his words. Somehow the hard *k* in the word *fuck* presses my horny button, and an ache pulses between my thighs.

I glance up. My eyes meet Luke's. He's clearly a few drinks deep, too, and I have to admit, I'm semi-inexperienced with a drunk Luke. As I recall, the times we've indulged to the point of excess have ended with either sex, a kiss, or something that leaves me completely and utterly confused.

I glance just beyond him and find not just my brother, but also my fiancé's brother. So Jack *is* on the guest list.

My eyes return to Luke. "Fancy meeting you here," I say, and he chuckles.

"Not many club options on the island."

"Did you find a strip club at least?" I ask.

He shakes his head. "Your brother found a hostess bar, which is essentially the same thing except it wasn't. Maui has some randomly strange laws."

I nod toward the dance floor where drunk people are still dancing sans drinks. "You mean like how you can't drink and dance at the same time?"

He laughs as his eyes follow the direction of my nod. "Yep, that would be one of them."

"That's why I'm standing here by the bar. Then I can get smashed, go dance, and come back for another when I'm ready to cool down."

"Brains and beauty," he says, and he leans forward and plants a kiss on my lips.

My heart races and every nerve in my body seems to light up at once as his mouth covers mine. I can't help it when I grab the back of his head and kiss him like I fucking mean it...because I *do* mean it. My tongue assaults his as he meets me step for step, and if this is just some show for his brother, well, I don't care.

His fingertips skate up my spine, and I shiver in his arms as I tighten my grip on him. I'm kissing Luke Dalton, and I'm in freaking Heaven.

Until Luke stops kissing me at the sound of Josh's voice.

"Get a room!" my brother yells, and I'm sure it's to break up what he thinks is a fake kiss just for show...but jeez, that sure didn't feel fake.

It felt real, and it felt hot, and it felt like holy hell I want more of it.

Nicki appears behind my brother, and she mock-smacks him in the back of the head. He rubs the spot of her offense, but he's laughing when he turns around and takes her in his arms.

Kaylee and Jack stand by a bit awkwardly in the presence of these other two happy couples, but I have a hard time recognizing that it's actually awkward because of the amount of rum I've consumed.

I drag Luke to the dance floor, where I promptly begin grinding on his leg, and it's all just so reminiscent of our first night together. That was back before we knew one another, back before we were roommates and before feelings were involved and before I knew who he really was. It was such a simple time compared to the mess that has ensued ever since.

We dance until the edges of sobriety seep back in, and then Luke has to use the restroom. I head back toward the bar to grab us each another round, and this time my big brother sidles up beside me just as I pick up my freshly poured mai tai.

"I know this is just pretend or whatever, but I have to tell you something," Josh says.

I glance over at him with raised brows that invite him to say whatever it is he needs to say as I sip the sweet liquid that's definitely going to leave me with a wicked headache in the morning.

"I'm pretty sure he's in love with you, Ellie."

Mai tai sprays out of my mouth.

"Classy," he mutters, pawing at his cheek.

"I'm sorry," I say. "But...what?"

"He's different around you. I saw him when he was with Michelle. He was never like this with her."

"Like what?" I ask. I go to take another sip, but Josh puts a hand on my forearm to stop my forward progress. Annoying, yes, but also probably necessary for him.

He shrugs. "I don't know. Happy? It's just the way he looks at you."

"It's an act, Josh. He doesn't want to be with me." I refrain from adding, *partly because of whatever you said to him*.

He shakes his head before he presses his lips together. "He's not that good of an actor."

My tummy somersaults at his words, and then Nicki drags him back to the dance floor. I'm left with that thought as I stand by the bar by myself trying to reconcile what I just heard from Josh with my actual feelings for Luke.

What if this whole time he's been hiding feelings for me, too? What if he's just been waiting for Josh to get back to clear things with his best friend before admitting how he really feels?

Or maybe Josh is just drunk, too. That's the more likely scenario.

I toss back the rest of my mai tai so I can return to the dance floor. I set my glass on the bar, and I haven't even turned around when a deep voice close to my ear sends shivers down my spine...and not the good kind. "Give up the act, Ellie. Don't marry him. I'm the better brother."

I turn to the side and raise a brow at Jack. Just as I open my mouth to tell him how much better Luke really is than him, he stops me.

"You can't deny there's something between us," he says.

My eyes are hot on his. *Is* there something here? Maybe. But would I ever do that to Luke?

Not on your life.

Jack thinks he can take what he wants, but I'm not like the others, as I've told Luke time and again. I will *never* bend for

Jack. Not when I'm so close to finally getting Luke to see that we could be everything together.

Jack's a little wasted, too, and he lowers his head toward me like he's moving in for a kiss as he loops an arm around my waist.

He may be charming. He may be sexy. He may be athletic and talented and rich and smell like a dream.

But he's also an asshole. He's rude and demeaning and crude. He takes what he wants without a care to who he might be hurting.

And the worst thing about him? He's not Luke.

I turn my head and move my face toward his ear. For a second, I'm sure he thinks I'm going to suck on his earlobe. I'm not.

Instead, I say directly into his ear, "You need to back off. I love Luke, and that's why I'm marrying him tomorrow. I'm not a pawn in your game. I'm your future sister-in-law."

Rather than listen to my words, he leans in and nuzzles my neck. I pull back out of his orbit, and when I do, I catch him looking with a sly smile over my shoulder.

I turn and follow his gaze, and when I see who he's smiling at, my heart drops.

Luke's staring at the two of us from halfway across the room in what had to look like a very compromising position as I nestled in close to his ear and Jack held me in his arms.

Luke purses his lips and shakes his head before he moves toward the door.

Does he really think I'd go for Jack? Even after the horse incident?

And then I realize...of course he thinks that. He'll *always* think he's going to lose to his brother because *he always has*.

But not this time.

"Shit," I mutter, and then I take off toward my fiancé so I can explain what he just saw.

CHAPTER 15

I find Luke waiting out front for a ride.

He gives me the kind of look that stops me a few feet away from him. I can't gauge his mood, not when there are so many variables at play. We're both a little drunk, emotions are high, we're getting married tomorrow...it's a lot.

But anger dominates as it seems to be vibrating off him.

"Figures this would be the time the car takes forever to pick me up," he mutters.

"I can explain whatever you think you just saw."

"Well if that isn't a textbook admission of guilt..." He glances away from me. "No need. This is all just for show. Right?"

I blow out a breath at the reminder. "I guess. I just..." I trail off. I just...*what?* I'm in love with Luke? I can't tell him that—not when he's been so clear that this is just a business deal to him. "I don't have any interest in your brother."

He huffs out a laugh. "Right. Because women are never interested."

I take a step closer to him, and then another step. I reach out and grab his hand. I squeeze it even though his remains limp, and part of me is touched that he cares while the other part of me thinks it's just because he's worried our little stunt here will go public.

"I'm not like the others, Luke," I say softly, repeating something I've told him before. "I see what he does. I see how your family treats you. I'd *never* give into him no matter how hard he tried."

"So he tried?" he asks flatly. "Again?"

I press my lips together in a non-answer that says everything.

He nods. "Okay," he says softly.

I squeeze his hand again. "I'd never do that to *you*. I'm on your side. Haven't you figured that out yet?"

"I don't need anybody on my side," he asserts.

"Okay," I say, doing my best to placate someone who's clearly angry and trying to hold it together as he awaits his car. And if I hadn't had five—or was it seven?—mai tais, I might be able to hold back from getting mad at him for the way he's acting. But I did have those drinks, and frustration permeates my blood.

"Fine. Push me away all you want," I spit at him. A dart of dizziness rushes through my head. I think I just need some water. I don't like fighting with Luke, but he keeps pushing me away and frankly I'm sick of it. "The fact of the matter is that we have to live together for at least the next year, and I'd rather do it on friendly terms than on whatever this is."

I spin on my heel to go back inside the club both to get some water and return to the girls who are probably still dancing as they wonder where the hell I went...and I come face to face with Kaylee.

All the blood drains from my face and that dizziness from a second ago gets a little stronger as my stomach heaves.

"Kaylee," I say, wondering exactly how much she just overheard as a buzz plays around my brain. I hear Luke mutter a curse word, but my stomach heaves again. "Uh..."

I'm about to ask her how much she overheard, but I'm never able to.

The mai tais catch up with me, and a second later, I'm heaving an embarrassing amount of liquid right into the hedges by the entrance to the club.

Well, I guess that's one way to avoid the conversation with Kaylee.

For now, anyway.

Luke's SUV arrives, and he helps me into the back. "Wait here," he says to the driver. He says something to Kaylee, and then he rushes back inside. He returns less than a minute later and hands me a bottle of water when he slides into the car.

I must pass out, because the next thing I know, sun streams through the curtains in our room and a pounding on the door matches the pounding in my head.

I'm in for a rude awakening in more ways than one.

"Don't do this," Kaylee says when I open the door. I glance around the suite, and I don't see Luke. He's not on the couch, the bathroom door is wide open, and his side of the bed is untouched. The balcony door is open, but I don't see him in either of the chairs out there, either, and it's pretty common for him to leave them open for both fresh air and the soundtrack of the ocean rolling in and out of the shore.

Maybe he went down for an early breakfast, and I don't even know where we left things. As I recall, though, we were in the middle of a pretty heated argument when I tossed my mai tais into the hedges.

"Don't do what?" I croak, my mouth dry from the amount of alcohol I consumed last night. I rustle through my suitcase for some ibuprofen.

"Marry my brother. If you don't love him...don't do it."

I find what I'm looking for and down three with nearly an entire bottle of water. There's no way my skin will have a dewy glow tonight for the wedding, not with rum sweating out of my pores. Six—or was it eight?—mai tais last night was a really dumb decision.

I sit on the couch and look up at my soon-to-be sister-in-law. It's not like I have anything else to lose at this point. He's not around to hear me, and if she runs to Luke with my confession, well, then one of two things will happen. Either he'll finally know the real truth rather than assuming it's just some little crush or he'll assume Kaylee is lying.

"That's the thing, Kaylee," I say softly. "I *do* love him."

Her brows dip. "But last night you said..."

I hold up a hand to stop her. "I'm in love with your brother. I'm not sure what you heard last night, but we'd both appreciate it if you could just keep whatever you think you heard to yourself."

She blows out a breath and walks over to the window. "You're asking me to choose between Luke and the rest of my family."

"No, I'm not," I say, and a wave of emotion plows through me. "I'm asking you to keep quiet about what you might've overheard. All that matters is that by the end of the day, I'll be married to the man I've fallen in love with. And whatever you overheard last night when we were fighting, that's the honest to God truth of the matter."

"But does he love you?" she asks.

"I like to think so," I say softly. And it's true. If nothing else, I think he's come to love me as a friend or maybe by default as the little sister of his best friend. Of course, in my wildest dreams, the things Josh said to me last night would be true—Luke would be in love with me, too.

Maybe I dreamed up that whole conversation. I was pretty drunk at the time.

I glance at the clock. "I have an appointment at the spa I need to get to. Please, please just be on Luke's side for this. He needs someone in his family who he can trust, and I'd love it if that person was you."

She purses her lips as she stares at me for a long beat. "I'll think about it. But Ellie, I need you to think about something, too. Whatever you're getting out of this, just be warned that you're also getting the Dalton last name. Sometimes it's cursed. Sometimes it isn't. If you're marrying my brother today, do it with that in mind. He never wanted to get married again, and there are reasons why."

"Thanks," I say simply, mostly because I don't know what else to say. She walks out the door, and I move toward the shower.

Except just as the door closes behind Kaylee, I hear a noise out on the balcony.

I turn to look in that direction, and that's when Luke appears in the doorway.

"You're in love with me?" he asks softly.

Always double check the balcony before you make big secret confessions, Ellie.

Always.

CHAPTER 16

"Yes. Yes, I have feelings for you. Yes I am in love with you. Yes it clouds everything and makes this an even dumber idea to actually marry you, but I'm doing it anyway whether or not you feel the same."

Do you feel the same?

I don't have the nerve to ask even though I just laid my entire heart on the line.

"Thank you," he says softly.

I try not to let it bother me that he doesn't immediately reciprocate my feelings. I've already locked into this for a year, so it doesn't matter. But I can't stop thinking how much better the next year will be if he *does* have feelings for me.

"Sure," I say awkwardly.

"Last night..." His eyes dip away from mine toward the floor and then out the window. "I wanted to tell you how much it hurt me to see you with my brother like that. I wanted to be pissed. I wanted to go back into that club and explode on my asshole brother. But then you got sick and I changed into a different person. I just needed to take care of you. To get you back here safe. It didn't matter what happened with Jack."

"Nothing happened with Jack," I say quietly.

He nods. "I know. But not because he didn't try." His eyes move back to mine. "So thank you."

"Sure," I say, and it's the second time I use that word in the span of a few seconds, and it's not any less awkward this time. I'm sure he has more to say, but I'm hungover and tired and just want to go shower to feel human again before we dig into all this. "Look, I need to take a shower, but I don't trust your sister. Or Jack. Or any of them, really."

There's a knock at our door.

"Then it's a good thing I have a plan," he says as he moves toward the door.

My brows dip down. "What plan?"

He opens the door, and a woman steps in.

"Alana?" I say, totally confused as to why she'd be here.

"Good morning," she says to both of us, and then she turns to my fiancé. "Luke, I got your message and rushed over here as soon as I could. What's going on?" she asks.

"We'd like to get married," Luke says.

Alana and I both regard him for a moment with confusion, and then Alana says, "Right. Tonight at six."

He shakes his head. "Before then."

My heart thumps in my chest. *What?* Somehow I manage to keep myself from reacting in front of Alana, though.

Luke shrugs. "Between my brother and his ego, her brother not wanting us to get married, and the media already sniffing around, we want a private ceremony so we're legally married before the one tonight at six. Then if anyone jumps in with whatever bombs they plan to detonate, it'll be too late."

She nods, and she holds a hand over her heart in an *oh-my-God-that's-so-romantic* kind of motion. "Of course, sir." Her eyes edge to me. "This is what you want, too?"

I force the confusion off my face. "Yes," I breathe, shocked that *this* is his plan but here for the ride anyway. What difference does a few hours make in the grand scheme of things? "Just give me an hour to make myself presentable."

Luke turns to me, and his eyes sweep over me. "You're perfect."

The words don't feel like an act when he says them with such warmth. He wouldn't *really* need to put on an act for Alana anyway...so is this real? Is he being sincere?

"I'm hungover and I just rolled out of bed," I counter.

Alana laughs. "You two are meant to be. I'll call Manny and make sure he can preside over your early ceremony, but I don't anticipate any problems. Would you like to do this here in your room?"

Luke nods. "Right over here," he says, nodding toward the slider doors that lead onto the balcony. "I'd say on the balcony, but we never know who's listening."

Alana nods and turns to leave.

"And Alana?" he says. She turns around. "Thank you."

She smiles. "Always happy to help a couple as in love as the two of you." She winks and heads out, and I'm about to run to the shower because holy shit, I'm getting married in an hour, when Luke stops me with a hand on my arm.

"Are you absolutely sure this is okay?" he asks me, his voice full of earnestness.

"Yes," I whisper. I nod resolutely. "I'm sure. There's no turning back now. I'm committed to this, and I will be here with you for the next year. We'll get that image turned around. We'll get through the birth of that baby. We'll get Michelle, Calvin, Savannah, and Todd off our backs. And in a year, this will all just be a distant memory."

I refrain from adding the parts about how my bank account will be a little more padded and my heart will be a little more cracked and how I don't *want* it to be a distant memory.

His eyes turn down to the ground. "Thank you," he murmurs. "Let's not tell a soul about this early version until after the wedding tonight, okay? I don't want it getting back to

Jack, or worse, to the media. There are too many ears always listening."

I loop my pinkie finger through his. "I pinkie promise."

* * *

I slip on a simple white dress I find in the hotel gift shop, allow my hair to fall straight down to the middle of my back, and brush on some light make-up. I don't look as disgusting as I did less than an hour ago, and I smell a hell of a lot better.

Alana knocks on the bedroom door of the suite, and I let her in without peeking out to see if Luke has changed. She hands me a small bouquet of colorful hibiscus flowers. "I took them from the hotel lobby. Don't tell anyone." Her eyes twinkle.

She agreed to be our witness, and only she, Manny, and the two of us know about this secret pre-wedding wedding ceremony. But this is the one that matters. This is the one that makes our union legal.

"Housekeeping is just finishing up out there," she says, and I nod. I take a few beats alone in the bathroom, spritz on a little perfume, and meet Alana back by the door that leads from the bedroom out to the main area of the suite.

"You ready for this?" she asks.

I force away the tears that spring to my eyes and draw in a deep breath. I never really thought I'd be doing this alone.

My mother may drive me crazy, but she's still my mother. My dad isn't here to walk me down the aisle. My brother, my best friend, other friends...none of them even know we're doing this.

It's just Luke and me.

There's something both romantic and terrifying about that.

"Ready," I say resolutely, and then she opens the door.

The suite has been transformed. Furniture has been moved, but that's not what strikes my attention first. It's the sheer amount of flowers and candles situated around the room, like Luke gave romance a real effort for this.

My heart squeezes.

My chest aches.

I take in the view of this room, the place where I'll take vows with another person that'll only really matter for the next year.

Alana moves first toward Manny, who stands with his back to the slider doors. Luke is on his left, and it's my turn to move my feet until I'm standing beside Luke.

The brightness of the sun is behind him from the angle where I stand, darkening his entire being into a shadow, and I can't help but pray that's not some sort of strange omen.

A song plays from someone's device somewhere as I start walking, just the slow keys of a piano, and it takes me a second to figure out that it's "Speechless" by Dan and Shay.

My hands tremble around the bouquet, and once I step into place beside Luke, I look up into his eyes.

I'm going to regret this.

I'm going to get hurt.

But I still want to do this.

For him.

Everything seems to fade away as our eyes meet, and despite the warnings in my own head about how I'm only going to come out the loser here, I don't care. I love him, and it's as simple and as complicated as that.

"Please join hands," Manny says. Alana reaches for my bouquet, and I pass it over.

Luke takes my hands in his. His are warm, and mine are ice cold.

"You look beautiful," he whispers. My lips tip up in a smile, and I'm about to tell him how freaking hot he looks in his charcoal shorts and black button-down shirt, but Manny cuts in before I get a chance to.

This feels like *us*, though. I'm in a simple dress. He's in something he might wear down to lunch. And maybe that's the thing—when it's for the two of us, it's pared down to the essentials. When it's a show for others, there's more that we're forced to put into it.

"We're gathered here today to unite Luke and Ellie in the bonds of matrimony," Manny says. "I'm going to give you the short version. Do you, Luke, take Ellie to be your lawfully wedded wife?"

"I do," Luke says.

"And do you, Ellie, take Luke to be your lawfully wedded husband?" Manny asks me.

I take a deep breath. "I do," I say on the exhale.

"Luke, please take the ring for Ellie and repeat after me." He gives Luke a beat to reach into his pocket for the ring, and then he continues. "Ellie, I give you this ring as a symbol of our union. With this ring, I thee wed."

Luke repeats the words as he slides on the diamond-encrusted band that fits with my engagement ring.

"And Ellie, Luke's ring?" he asks me. Alana hands it to me. "Repeat after me. Luke, I give you this ring as a symbol of our union. With this ring, I thee wed."

I repeat his words.

"You have consented to matrimony and both Alana and I have witnessed this exchange," Manny says. "By the authority vested in me by the state of Hawaii, I now pronounce you husband and wife. Noho me ka hau'oli," he says in Hawaiian, and then in English, "Be happy."

Luke's lips spread into a smile, and I can't help when mine do, too. He leans forward and plants a gentle kiss on my mouth. It may be soft, and it may be simple, but it's everything. It lights me up from the inside. I want more. I want *everything*, and I want it with Luke.

Is that too much to ask?

CHAPTER 17

"You're sure you want to do this?" Josh asks. He's playing it off like a normal wedding day question to the bride from her big brother in front of the women working on Nicki and me, but we both know what he's really asking.

I can't help but find the irony in the fact that I had to convince both Josh and Nicki they wanted to get married on their wedding day while they're trying to convince me of the opposite.

I don't dare open my eyes as the make-up artist, Leila, dusts a shimmery shadow over them. Nicki is getting her hair done a few feet away by Mia. "Positive."

"Then I won't stop you."

I feel Leila step away, and I open my eyes. "Thank you," I murmur.

He gives me a sad smile. "Mom and Dad are gonna be pissed that I was here and they weren't."

I press my lips together. "Yeah," I say. I don't know what else to say. Would they really want to be present for their daughter's first wedding even though it's fake? Or does this whole thing appear a certain way because of the very fact that they aren't here?

"Just be careful," he says quietly.

"He's *your* best friend, Josh. You're the one who brought us together in the first place. Remember?"

He chuckles. "That's not what I heard from Nicki."

My cheeks flame. "She told you?"

"Of course she did." He reaches for my hand and squeezes it. "Take care of him, and take care of yourself, too."

"We're fine," I say, but his kind words are kind of making me feel like that's not entirely true. *I am not fine, and I'm willing to bet Luke isn't, either.* "Now go and talk to him, too. The guy who never wanted to get married again probably needs his best friend more than ever."

He nods. "See you out there," he says.

"I'll be the one in white."

He snort-laughs. "Like you can really get away with wearing white to your wedding."

I offer him a glare and a middle finger, and he leaves his echoes of laughter behind as he walks out of the room.

Nicki squeezes my hand as Mia and Leila talk to each other a few feet away. "You handled that well, but now it's time to be honest with me," she says softly so the two women don't overhear whatever she's about to say. "Are you sure you really want to go through with this?"

I want to tell her I've already done it. So badly. She's my best friend, and I tell her everything.

Is there really any reason not to?

Just one.

Luke told me not to tell a soul.

Leila and Mia may seem like they're not listening a few feet away from us...but that doesn't mean they won't hear me.

I keep my trap shut even though it's one of the hardest things I've ever had to do.

I'm *married*. It's a crazy thing to believe. I'm somebody's *wife*.

If you would've told me that I'd be married by the end of June when Belinda walked into Todd's office in Chicago and caught me just as I crashed into an orgasm, I never would've believed it.

And it doesn't really matter *why* I'm married. The fact is that I'm now Mrs. Luke Dalton.

There's a knock at the door, and Nicki runs to answer it. Mia puts a few extra pins in my hair to make sure it's secure, but I'm just about at the point where all I have to do is slip into my dress, buckle my shoes, and put on my jewelry.

Kaylee appears in the doorway. "Can I talk to you?" she asks. She glances at the women packing up their supplies. "Alone?"

I nod. "Can you excuse us, please?" I say to the women, and Mia closes the door behind the two of them as they walk out to join Nicki in the suite. "What's wrong, Kaylee?"

"Don't do this," she pleads. "Don't go through with it. Don't make me choose between keeping your secrets and telling my family the truth."

"Kaylee..." I start, not exactly sure where I'm going with that but sure I don't want to have this conversation. It's too late, anyway. *We're already married. We've already done it.* "You're not keeping secrets. I love him."

"If you love him, think about *him*. He might be my older brother, but he's the one who needs protecting right now. I don't know what your motivation is, or even what his is, really, but there has to be some other way to solve whatever the problem is aside from what you're doing."

"You're absolutely right," I say, surprised we agree on something here. "He does need protecting. From your brother. From your parents. From the ex-wife and the ex-girlfriend trying to drain the life out of him. He has taken care of me, and I'm going to take care of him, too."

That's a promise.

She stares at me for a beat.

"Look, Kaylee. I love him. That's what matters. Why does it matter to you?"

"I told you earlier, there are curses with family you don't want to get mixed into. Especially in your line of work. If the truth came out, they'd both be in trouble, and a simple Instagram post sure as hell isn't going to fix it." Her arms are crossed and one brow is raised as she snarls at me.

"Thanks for the warning, but I can take care of myself. And my soon to be husband." My voice is full of a certainty I'm not sure I feel. "Now I need to get dressed. You can see yourself out."

She purses her lips at me with a glare before she spins on her heel and walks out, and damn it all, I thought she was the one who was supposed to be on Luke's side.

It sure as hell doesn't feel like it. If anything, it feels like Luke and I are in this alone. Just one more thing to bond me to my new husband, I guess.

I don't know if she's running off to tell Jack what she thinks she heard or if she's running to the media, and I don't know *why* she'd do that if she wants to protect her brother. Either way, I'm vibrating with anger.

I have to brush it off, though. I have to appear as the glowing bride because I'm about to walk down the aisle. Even though we're already married, this is the one we'll post pictures of. We didn't even actually *take* any photos at our real ceremony.

This one is the one for show, though. This time, the staff photographer at our hotel will take photos so we can sell them to the highest bidder when the media gets wind of our nuptials...if they haven't already.

CHAPTER 18

"You're a glowing bride," Nicki says with a smile as her eyes sweep down my white lace, chiffon, and satin gown. The top is a gorgeous lacy design with v-neck that fades into a simple bottom with a slit. "If I didn't know the truth, I'd really believe it."

I glance at her. "It's real for me, even if we're not at the marriage stage yet in real time."

"I know it is," she says softly. "And maybe you'll get there."

I nod and press my lips together as I try to ward off the sudden heat pricking behind my eyes.

"You ready for this?" We're standing by the pool, just out of sight from those gathered to witness our little event.

I nod. "This is just a formality at this point," I say.

Her brows dip down. "Because it's fake?"

I press my lips into a small smile and shake my head. I can tell her now, right? There's nobody around us really, and we're seconds away from doing this in front of everybody anyway. "Because we're already married."

This time her brows arch up nearly off her forehead. "What?"

I smile. "We did it this morning in our suite. We didn't want to take any chances that the media would find out before we made it legal."

She smacks me in the arm. "And you didn't tell me?"

"I couldn't. My husband made me promise."

Alana comes rushing up to us. "Nicki, you're up," she says, panting like she was trying to wave us down but we missed it due to my big confession.

Nicki narrows her eyes at me. "All right, girlfriend. Let's do this, but later we're going to have to have a chat about how you don't keep these big things from your best friend."

I laugh as she hustles to get into place. "The last time I told you a secret, Josh knew three seconds later," I remind her, and she giggles as she starts her walk toward the aisle.

And then I'm by myself for a beat before Alana will prompt me to start walking.

I don't have to question whether what I'm doing is right since it's already done, and that helps push away any nerves I might've felt in doing this.

I wish my parents were here, but since the *actual* wedding already took place and *nobody* was there, I don't suppose it really matters.

I try to get a glimpse ahead, but I'm around the corner and out of sight so nobody will see me per wedding traditions.

I wonder who's gathered there on the beach, whether Luke called in any more surprises, whether Jack will be sitting there exuding all that sexual energy in my direction like he always does even though I'm literally standing there marrying his brother.

"We made it!" a familiar voice behind me calls in victory. "She's right there."

It can't be.

I turn slowly around and spot two people rushing toward me.

"Dad?" I say softly, those tears pinching behind my eyes again. "Mom?"

"Oh honey," my mom says, and she flies into my arms.

I can't cry. It'll ruin my make-up.

But dammit, my freaking parents are here. This is bigger than just Luke and me and some ridiculous plan. Did Josh invite them here...or did Luke?

Because if it was Josh, well, that's one thing. But if it was Luke...maybe that means something.

It's just a show for the media. For Jack. For the Daltons. That's one possible meaning.

But another possible meaning is that he listened to me. He saw that I had nobody here and he called in Josh and Nicki, and it doesn't feel like that was just for the media or just for show. It feels like it was just for me.

What if he did this, too? Does that mean he cares?

"Luke told us everything," my mom says softly. "And we don't understand the reasons, but you're our little girl, and we will always, *always* support you."

That.

That right there is *family*.

They're not here to talk me out of it. They're here to stand by my side and support me.

I wish Luke had that, too. And he will, now that he's married to me.

"I couldn't let you walk down the aisle alone," my dad says, and those damn tears tip over and I just cross my fingers that I don't have runny mascara raccoon eyes.

"I love you guys," I say to my parents, and they take turns hugging me before they each grab onto one of my arms and Alana signals us to start walking down the aisle.

It's exactly like I pictured my dream beach wedding.

Well, *almost* exactly.

I'm sort of missing the guy who's madly in love with me and the majority of our closest friends and extended families, but at least I have my dad to walk me down the aisle.

Everything else, though? Spot on, from the magical glow of the sun as it descends into the ocean to the calm, rolling tranquility of the waves, to the prince standing up front as he waits for me to walk down the aisle.

I thought I'd be walking by myself.

I thought nobody would be giving me away, and not in some statement of independence on my part, but rather the idea of chucking tradition since this isn't real anyway.

As soon as I turn the corner, I find him in the small group gathered...but then my eyes always seem to search him out. It's as if nobody else is here, and maybe they aren't. I wouldn't know because I can't look away from him, and tears prick behind my eyes yet again when his meet mine. I sense a bit of awe, a bit of wonder...and maybe some heat, maybe some love—or at least some sort of affection. He *has* to at least care about me, right?

I dissect the possibility of heat in his eyes. I certainly look different from the first time we did this just a few hours ago after being pampered and styled by an entire team, but he does, too.

He wears a dark khaki linen suit with a white shirt underneath, his tan skin glowing and his blue eyes shining as he waits for me to walk to him. I move slowly as the same song as earlier plays, and somehow I feel a little speechless myself as I stare into the eyes of the guy who will play the part of my husband for the next year.

A dart of sadness streaks through my chest at the thought of actually parting when this next year is up. And then another pang of sadness creeps in, but unlike the first streak...this one sticks.

It's not like we can't still be friends when it's over, but it means I'll have to move out of the Barbie dreamhouse. It means the fantasy will be over. It means reality will kick in again and I can resume my hunt for Prince Charming.

He's told me time and again it's not him. But when I look at him...I still see the prince. I'm not convinced that he isn't. I still hold onto the night we met, that night when he made me laugh and feel safe even though we were strangers and he pushed my body past any sort of pleasure that it had ever felt before. He was a prince to me that night, but nobody's perfect—not even Prince Charming. I bet even *he* had a past. Even *he* must have made poor decisions or acted out of jealousy or made the princess cry.

I swipe at the tears as they stream down my cheeks. I offer a smile and play them off as happy tears since this is supposed to be the happiest moment of my life.

It's not.

When I join Luke in front of Manny, he stares at me. His eyes don't flick from mine—not even to greet my parents. That just causes another surge of emotion to course through me.

"Welcome friends," Manny says. "We are gathered here today to unite Luke and Ellie in the bonds of matrimony. Who gives this woman to be married?"

"Her mother and I do," my dad says, his voice wavering with emotion, and for a split second I think what we're doing here is all wrong. My even-keel dad rarely shows emotion, and I feel like a huge disappointment to my family as I take vows to someone knowing this is only temporary—knowing that *my parents* know this is only temporary.

But then I look into Luke's eyes as my parents back away, and somehow everything seems right again. He thumbs a tear from my cheek before he takes my hands in his. My smile is genuine through my sadness. I'm happy to be here with him, truly—I just wish there could be a different ending for us...a fairy tale ending.

Manny begins the ceremony. "This is not the beginning of Luke and Ellie's story but rather an acknowledgement of the next chapter they will write together. These bonds are not to be taken lightly, and today they will affirm their relationship both formally and publicly. In Hawaii, we say E hele me ka pu'olo, and that means you make every person, place, or condition better than before, always. This is the sacred Hawaiian way, and as we witness the union here today, we can see that Ellie and Luke make each other better than before."

Luke leans over and presses a soft kiss to my cheek. I'm not sure if it's for show or if it's a rare expression of emotion, a way of thanking me for what I'm doing. I hope I'm leaving *him* in a better place than he was before. I hope what we're doing right now is for the overall good. But I'm still certain I'm going to regret it.

"With that in mind, if anyone objects to this union, speak now or forever hold your peace."

I hold my breath as my worried eyes meet Luke's during Manny's ridiculously long pause. I can't bear to look out over those gathered here. I'm sure Kaylee has objections—unless Luke got to her. Jack has objections. Even Carol and Tim do, and Josh and Nicki and my parents. And that's it. That's everybody that's here—at least I *think* that's it. And I *think* they're all here, but I'm not really sure. My eyes locked up on Luke's when I walked in and I never looked to see.

It would be far too cliché for someone to actually stand up and object at this point, wouldn't it? We already know everyone here has their doubts. We probably should've had the foresight to tell Manny not to include that particular line in the script. Their objections don't really matter, anyway, since we've already done this.

Fair GAME

"With no objections to this union, the happy couple will now make their vows," Manny says, and I finally exhale. Luke does, too—visibly.

We're past the scary part. It's smooth sailing from here...right? In someone else's story, maybe. Not in mine.

"Luke, do you take Ellie to be your lawfully wedded wife and equal partner, to join with her and share with her all that is to come, and to commit to a life together from now until you part?" Manny asks.

We were careful about keeping that whole *until death do us part* thing out of our vows. Nothing Manny just said is a lie. We both know what we're vowing to here, and when we *part* in a year, we'll both be able to say that we stayed true to our vows.

Hopefully, anyway. I don't plan on taking on any other *partners* in the next year, and I don't think he does, either.

"I do," Luke says.

Manny turns to me, "And Ellie, do you take Luke—"

"Stop!" a woman's voice yells. It's out of breath and loud and screeches Manny's sentence to a halt as we all freeze.

I spot the look of horror on Luke's face as he turns his head before I do in the split half-second it takes for me to turn my head and see a woman running down the aisle toward us. Jack steps out into the aisle with a broad, sly smile on his face. And when my eyes fall on the woman who rushes up toward Jack's side, a pit forms deep in my stomach.

The woman holds a hand over her stomach as she moves toward us, and I'm about to glance over at Luke to gauge his reaction when she yells again.

"Stop the wedding!"

The entire wedding party sits in stunned silence, and then Luke hisses a single word: "Michelle."

To be continued in Book 4, **WAITING GAME.**

ACKNOWLEDGMENTS

Thank you to my husband for everything you do. The support, encouragement, and love is what makes this possible. Thank you to my kids for nap time and quiet time when mommy gets to write, and thank you to my parents who love hanging out with my babies so I can get some computer time in.

Thank you to Trenda London from It's Your Story Content Editing, Diane Holtry and Alissa Riker for beta reading, Najla Qamber for the gorgeous cover design, and Katie Harder-Schauer from Proofreading by Katie.

Thank you to Wildfire Marketing, my ARC team, Team LS, and all the bloggers who read, post, and review.

Thank you to you, the reader, for taking time out of your life to spend it with Ellie. I hope you enjoyed what you read, and I can't wait for you to read the next book.

xoxo,
Lisa Suzanne

ABOUT THE AUTHOR

Lisa Suzanne is a romance author who resides in Arizona with her husband and two kids. She's a former high school English teacher and college composition instructor. When she's not cuddling or chasing her kids, she can be found working on her latest book or watching reruns of *Friends*.

ALSO BY LISA SUZANNE

A LITTLE LIKE DESTINY
A Little Like Destiny Book One
#1 Bestselling Rock Star Romance

TAKE MY HEART
My Favorite Band Book One
#1 Bestselling Rock Star Romance